# MISCONCEPTION

BY
LIV CONSTANTINE

Other books by Liv Constantine

*The Last Mrs. Parrish*
*The First Shot - Novella Prequel to The Last Mrs. Parrish*
*The Last Time I Saw You*
*The Wife Stalker*
*The Stranger in the Mirror*
*The Senator's Wife*

# Chapter One
## Iris

Iris Thomas had been dreading the party all week. Now that the day was here, she forced herself to smile at Molly, her seven-year-old stepdaughter, as the little girl twirled around in her purple Rapunzel costume. Molly took a little bow as if for an audience. She had costumes for all the Disney princesses, and was thrilled that the theme of today's birthday party allowed her to dress as the princess of her choice.

"Iris, is my hair as pretty as Rapunzel's?" she asked, running a hand through her blond curls.

"Prettier!" Iris told her.

"I can't wait 'til Bailey sees what we got her! She's gonna love it," Molly exclaimed, running to her dresser and picking up the gift wrapped in pink-and-white balloon paper. Molly had insisted that they buy the light-up karaoke machine she'd spotted at the toy store. It would be a hit with Bailey—her parents, not so much. "Is it almost time to go to the party?"

Bailey, who was celebrating her seventh birthday today, was Molly's best friend. The two had met at the beginning of second grade, only three months ago, but were now inseparable. Iris would have been thrilled for Molly to make such a good friend, and so quickly, at her new school, if only it had been anyone other than Bailey McBride.

Beardsley-Arms, an elite private school in Los Angeles, counted among its students the offspring of the very rich and very famous. Iris and her husband were neither, but they both did well enough to send Molly to the highly rated school. Iris had been a little concerned that she might feel out of her league, but Alan was determined to transfer Molly there from her last school, which had larger class sizes and a less-effective student-teacher ratio. And it was, after all, Alan's decision, as Iris had become Molly's stepmother only a year ago. Iris looked at her watch, trying to quell the sinking feeling in her stomach.

"Yes, it's almost time, sweetie. I'm going to get changed now and then we'll leave."

Of all weekends for Alan to be away, why did it have to be now, she thought, as she rifled through her clothes closet, searching for the right thing to wear. Alan was in Brazil shooting for his documentary on the South American rain forest and wouldn't return until late tonight. She grabbed her cell phone from the nightstand and hit the contact for her sister.

"Hey, girl, what's going on?" Violet's voice came over the line.

"Ugh. I knew I should have gotten something new for today. I have nothing to wear."

"What are you talking about? I though we agreed on your Frame flare jeans and a black tee."

Iris sank down on the bed and sighed. "We did. But you know all the other moms are going to be in their designer best and swimming in diamonds and gold. I'm going to look like some hick from nowhere, and Sasha's going to look runway ready."

Violet laughed. "You *are* a hick from nowhere. But seriously, you'll look great in anything. Don't let those posers make you feel bad about yourself."

"I know, you're right. But I haven't seen either of them since . . ." She had to think. When had she last seen Bailey's parents? "Oh yeah, since Alan and I ran into them at Nobu a few months ago. I can't believe I have to spend an entire day at their *fantabulous* beach house. And without Alan."

"Can't you drop Molly off? You have to stay?"

"They're seven." The invitation specified either a parent or nanny was required. "Maybe I should have hired someone just for today," she said, only half joking. Why hadn't she thought of that sooner?

"You'll be fine. Hold your head up. You're not the one with anything to be ashamed of. Call me the minute you get home."

"I will. Thanks. Love ya."

She pulled her jeans from the shelf and slipped them on. Sighing, she grabbed a handful of tops, trying on one after another. She glanced at her Apple Watch to check the temperature: seventy-three and sunny, a perfect November day in Southern California. Finally, she plucked the black Tom Ford T-shirt from the back of her closet and stared at it. It was the only designer item she still owned. She'd bought it on a whim one day—the day she'd gone on a desperate shopping spree after getting another negative pregnancy test result. She had really believed it would work that time, had even imagined that she felt the subtle changes in her body already. But forty thousand dollars down the drain and countless needles and procedures later, she was still very much not pregnant. She'd never worn the eleven-hundred-dollar shirt but had kept it as a reminder that money couldn't buy happiness. Today, though, it might help her to stand out a little bit less, so she pulled it over her head, fluffed her hair, and went to find Molly.

"Ready, Molly?" she called, going into her bedroom.

"Yay! It's time?" She got up from the floor, where she'd been lounging with their year-old yellow Lab. "Bye, Oscar. I'll bring you some cake!" Her stepdaughter's blue eyes shone with delight, and her adorable, freckled nose crinkled in that endearing way that warmed Iris's heart every time.

After Molly buckled herself in the back seat, Iris backed the Audi Q7 out of the driveway and mentally prepared herself for the torturous afternoon ahead. Over the past six years, she'd done her best to forget about the McBrides, but the fact that Donny was the current heartthrob on the increasingly popular TV series *Santa Barbara Medical* made that impossible. He and Sasha were constantly popping up in her Instagram feed—the perfect little family. No one would ever imagine them capable of the deception and betrayal that brought them together. There was no escaping them; even in the grocery store, their faces stared back at her from the covers of celebrity magazines. Iris and Alan traveled in completely different social circles from the McBrides, and so she had been spared running into them. Until now. Their daughter, Bailey, had changed all of that.

# MISCONCEPTION

The drive from Iris's home in Santa Monica to Malibu took a good half hour, and when they arrived, she felt the lump in her throat grow larger. She'd looked the house up online. Over two acres of prime beachfront property with a private tennis court, an infinity pool overlooking the ocean, multilevel decks, and Zen-like walkways meandering through lush vegetation. All this for the bargain price of thirty-five million dollars.

"Oh, look," Molly exclaimed as the car approached the house. Over the arched gates was an enormous balloon rainbow, and signs with pink twinkling lights reading *Happy Birthday, Bailey* hung on each side of the entrance. Iris inched the Audi down the long driveway and into a motor court where other cars were already parked. Blowing out a breath, she unbuckled and pasted a smile on her face.

"Ready, Molly?" she called, but Molly was already pushing the door open with an excited cry. The house was huge, more like a small hotel, and Iris's first thought was how hard it must be to keep it all clean. But of course they would have help for that.

"Come on, Iris! Hurry up," Molly scolded, and Iris picked up her pace, her sense of dread increasing with every step. The door opened, and a young woman dressed as Princess Jasmine greeted them. "Hello, and welcome. Today is Disney Princess Day, and we're going to have so much fun." She handed Molly a white tote bag with all the princesses and Molly's name embroidered in bright-colored stitches.

The young woman crouched down and smiled at Molly. "Inside your bag is a bathing suit, goggles, and a towel for later. And lots of other fun goodies too. Follow me to the party."

"Thank you," Molly said, her eyes wide as she looked from the woman to the bag while they walked. "Look, Iris, a Nintendo Switch!" She held up the bright pink console, and Iris gasped despite herself. A two-hundred-dollar party favor?

"Why don't you let me hold onto your bag. Here's Bailey's gift. You bring it in to give to her." Iris traded items with her and snuck a quick look inside the bag, seeing that the bathing suit was a yellow, white, and pink Givenchy one-piece. Sasha had certainly gone all out on the goodie bags. Iris bet that by the time she tallied everything up, the total would be close to a thousand dollars—for a seven-year-old's birthday party!

They moved quickly through the two-story entrance hall, and Iris couldn't take her eyes off of the floor-to-ceiling crystal chandelier. It was so over the top, even a bit bizarre, and had probably cost a small fortune. The house itself was a mass of white—white walls, white marble, white furniture, and dramatic high ceilings. It had to be the coldest house she'd ever seen, but it had certainly been built to impress. Through French doors to the wide deck overlooking the ocean, more balloons and decorations celebrating Bailey were everywhere, and plush child-size chairs and sofas surrounded a play area with racks of princess costumes, tiaras, kids' makeup, and fancy jewelry. Iris spotted four other hired princesses roving around, and in one corner there was a cotton candy stand, in another a sundae and soda fountain with little stools around it. As if that weren't enough, a long table held bowl after bowl of different candy, behind which more adult princesses stood, ready to scoop it out into princess-themed plastic bags. Unbelievable.

For the adults, there was a champagne fountain, roving waitstaff with wine, assorted appetizers, as well as a fully staffed full bar. If this was how they threw a birthday party for their seven-year-old, she couldn't imagine what the sweet sixteen would look like. She finished her glass of wine, and gratefully accepted another from the waiter instantly at her side.

There were already children playing together, and a small cluster of five moms chatting and sipping wine. Just as she'd expected, their outfits, though casual, were clearly not off the rack. Perfect hair, manicured and pedicured, impossibly smooth-skinned, with smiles revealing brilliant white teeth, the women were toned and polished to perfection. One, an actress Iris recognized instantly, looked twenty pounds lighter than she did on the big screen.

"Molleeeeee!" a young girl with long brown hair squealed, running up to Iris's stepdaughter and enveloping her in a bear hug. "You're here! Come look at my cake." She grabbed Molly's hand and pulled her down the stairs to the infinity pool on the lower deck. Iris had never met Bailey before. Their school discouraged parents from any class participation, believing second grade was the point at which children needed to become more independent. The girls had been itching for playdates since the start of school, but it hadn't happened yet. The first time Molly had asked, Iris called Sasha, and the two of them agreed that playdates for Molly and Bailey were out of the question. But over time, Iris realized they couldn't put the girls off for long.

Iris made her way over to the group of women. The conversation stopped as she approached, and they turned to look at her.

"Hello, I'm Iris Thomas, Molly's stepmother," she introduced herself.

"I'm Rowan Melnick," the one with red hair and luminous green eyes said, and when Iris heard the name, she realized Rowan must be the wife of director Brian Melnick.

The others chimed in, but the actress simply smiled and nodded at Iris, as if there were no need to introduce herself—who wouldn't know who she was? They picked back up on their conversation, mentioning names Iris had heard of and movie projects in the works. She was feeling like a fifth wheel when suddenly she saw Sylvia, one of the moms from Molly's class. At least there was one friendly face.

"Sylvia, nice to see you," Iris said, walking away from the group and toward the woman who had always been warm and approachable. Sylvia's daughter, Teagan, was the youngest of seven children, the other six the product of her producer father's various marriages and relationships.

"Hi, Iris. I saw Molly. She looks adorable in her Rapunzel dress." Sylvia glanced around, smiling. "Quite a party, don't you think? Sasha pulled out all the stops."

"Yes," Iris said.

"Well, I'm going to make the rounds . . . Have you seen Sasha yet?" she asked.

"No, I haven't," Iris said, and Sylvia moved away to meld into the group still huddled together and laughing.

As if the mention of her name had conjured her, there she was. Sasha. She sauntered over, looking gorgeous in an emerald jumpsuit, not a black hair out of place, and stopped in front of Iris. "Hello, Iris. So nice to see you."

Before she could respond, Donny joined his wife and slid an arm around her waist. He looked expensive, his thick black hair slicked back and his brown eyes as captivating as ever.

"You're looking well, Iris," he said.

"Thank you" was the only thing she could manage as she stared back at her ex-husband, wishing she were anywhere but here.

# Chapter Two
## Sasha

Sasha poured herself a glass of wine and took a seat next to Donny out on the deck. She'd thought the party would never end and was relieved to have all those screaming children finally gone. Taking a long sip, she leaned back and closed her eyes, breathing in the cool evening air, and felt herself relax. "I think Bailey had a good time, don't you?" she asked, her eyes still shut.

"The party was a singular success. Great job, Dr. Everett," Donny said. Sasha smiled and looked at her husband. He played a doctor on television, but she was the real deal. It was, in fact, how they'd met. His show had hired her to consult on a story line. And she knew the moment she saw Donny that she had to have him.

"Angela said Bailey fell asleep before she got through the second bedtime story," she told him. Angela, their nanny, was a godsend. She was a miracle worker with Bailey, who could be a real handful—strong-willed and constantly in motion. Sasha found her utterly exhausting. She was a sweet child, beautiful too, but Sasha wished she were just a little less boisterous and more demure. Angela knew how to channel Bailey's energy so that by the time Sasha was home from work, she was tired and more manageable. Angela had recently taught Bailey how to paddleboard, and Sasha had been pleased, but somewhat surprised, that the chubby Angela was so athletic. They'd been through quite a few nannies before Angela, for various reasons. The last one had gotten a little too friendly with Donny, and that's when Sasha had decided that the next nanny they hired would be older and unattractive. It was bad enough that Donny was surrounded by beautiful women on set all day. When he came home, the only beauty he was going to see was her. Angela was perfect—late forties, frumpy, a little overweight, and completely dedicated to Bailey. Sasha would never have to worry about Donny sneaking into Angela's room at night.

"I'm still surprised that Iris actually showed up. I thought she'd send Molly with a sitter or something." Sasha knew that Iris didn't have a nanny—Angela had told her that Molly was picked up and dropped off by Iris herself every day. She was probably the only mom at school who drove her own child. And Molly wasn't even really hers. Maybe she was trying to prove something to her husband. Sasha knew it couldn't be about money. Donny had been generous with the divorce settlement, and Iris's new husband was a well-known writer and producer of documentaries. But then again, Iris had always been uncomfortable living in the world of the one percent. That was one of the reasons Donny got tired of her. She wasn't cut out to be the wife of a famous actor.

"She seems to be doing well. I'm glad," he said.

Sasha shot Donny a look. What the hell did that mean? "Excuse me?"

He sighed. "Come on, Sash, don't you feel just a little bad about the way things happened?"

She gave him a cold look. "Are you saying you're sorry? Do you

12

wish you were still with her?"

He reached out and took her hand in his. "Of course not. I'm just saying we have everything, and she never got . . . I mean, she never had a child. I love you, and I love our life. I just wish Iris hadn't been collateral damage."

Sasha had to bite her lip to keep from saying the wrong thing. She'd known it was a mistake to let Iris back into their lives. She would never admit it to Donny, but Iris *had* looked great at the party. Not as great as Sasha, of course, but still. And now Donny's guilt was resurfacing. Sasha thought they were done with all that, that Donny had finally put it behind him. Iris had always made herself out to be the good one, the poor innocent victim, and now she was doing it again, even after remarrying. When Bailey had first told Sasha about her new friend, Molly, Sasha had done everything in her power to discourage the friendship. When Iris had called her, they agreed it was better to keep the girls apart. Sasha had even tried to have Molly moved into a different class, but that hadn't worked, even when she'd offered a generous donation to the school—a thinly disguised bribe. But there was so much money floating around that it didn't make a difference, and she'd only made herself look foolish. Then goody two-shoes Iris had called last week. Sasha thought back to the conversation.

"Obviously this is awkward, but it's not really fair to the girls to let our history prevent them from spending time together," Iris had said.

Sasha was taken off guard. She hadn't wanted to sound petty, but she didn't give a crap about denying Bailey and Molly's friendship. They were seven—they'd get over it. "I'm not sure it's a great idea to encourage their friendship. I mean, can I really trust you not to bad-mouth Donny in front of his daughter?"

There had been stunned silence on the other end of the phone. Finally, Iris spoke again, this time in clipped tones. "I would never do that. What kind of a . . . Listen, Sasha, you're the last person I ever wanted to speak with again, but I am willing to put my personal feelings aside for the sake of my daughter."

"Don't you mean your stepdaughter?" Sasha couldn't help saying, knowing it would wound her to the core.

Iris hadn't risen to the bait. "What do you say, Sasha? Can we put our differences aside for the sake of the girls?"

"Yes, of course. I would do anything for my daughter. I'll add Molly's name to the birthday party list, and you can coordinate future playdates with Angela, our nanny."

Donny's voice interrupted her thoughts. "I've upset you. I'm sorry. I guess it was a little jarring seeing her again after all this time."

"I understand," Sasha said in a sweet voice. "You're such a darling to care about everyone's feelings. But you don't have to worry about Iris. She's deliriously happy. Even told me how much happier she is being out of the limelight and married to someone with a serious job." A complete lie, of course.

Donny looked hurt. "She said that? A serious job?"

Sasha laughed. "You know she's a bit of an intellectual snob. You told me yourself that she never took actors seriously. If she can't

14

see how insanely smart and talented you are, that's her problem." She could tell she'd hit her mark. Donny wrapped his arms around her.

"I love you."

"And I love you. We're perfect together."

She pushed him back down in his chair and stood up, leaning in to kiss him, then unzipped his pants. She wore nothing under her robe, and he sucked in a breath as she straddled his lap. They began to move together, and with every thrust she knew she was pushing Iris further and further from his mind.

# Chapter Three
## Iris

After she put an exhausted Molly to bed, Iris called her sister.

"How bad was it?" Violet asked.

"Oh, Vi, even worse than I thought." After she listened to Iris fill her in on the over-the-top party, Violet asked the question Iris knew she'd been dying to ask.

"How was it seeing them together? Did it bring it all back?"

Iris sighed. "I don't know. She's just horrible. She was all over him any time I came near. Like she was marking her territory or something. As if *I'm* the one who stole *her* man. I just wish Alan had been with me."

Iris heard a scream come from Molly's bedroom. "Gotta go, Molly's having another nightmare." She disconnected and ran to the child's room.

Molly was writhing back and forth. "Mommy, Mommy! No!"

Iris gently roused her. "Honey, wake up. You're having a bad dream."

Molly's eyes flew open, and tears ran down her cheeks.

Iris leaned in to hug her, but Molly pushed her away, her little fists pummeling her. "You're not my mommy. I want my mommy!"

"I'm sorry, sweetie. What can I do?"

"Where's Daddy? I want Daddy!" she began to wail again, and the sight broke Iris's heart.

"He'll be home in a little while."

Molly grabbed her stuffed lion and hugged it to her chest, turning on her side, away from Iris. "Go away."

She rose from the bed. "Just call me if you need anything," she said as she retreated from the room.

Molly's nightmares were getting worse. It pained Iris that the child kept pushing her away. Linda had been gone for two years now, since Molly was only five. According to Alan, the nightmares were a problem at first, but they'd all but stopped until he married Iris. It didn't take an expert to see that his remarriage had awakened in Molly the trauma of the accident and her mother's death. Iris had been naïve to think that she was walking into a ready-made family. She'd known that Molly would take time to adjust, to accept Iris's role in her life, but she hadn't been prepared for the depth of the child's grief and her inability to do anything to help.

She glanced at the clock on the microwave. Alan would be home soon. She made herself a cup of tea and sat replaying the evening over again in her mind. She thought about her sister's question. It *had* been hard seeing them together. It wasn't that she missed Donny. She didn't. Her mother had warned her not to marry an actor, that they could be egotistical and self-centered, but she hadn't listened. And when they first got together, Donny a bartender, she a graduate student, he was everything she wanted in a man. Smart, funny, kind, considerate. The first two might still be true, but as his star rose, his good qualities diminished, and by the time he left, she barely recognized him anymore.

18

She thought back to the night Donny had come home to tell her he was leaving. She'd had a speech all prepared about how they should give in vitro one last try, even though they'd agreed that if this last one didn't work, they'd look into adoption. But she wasn't ready to throw in the towel, despite the fact that forty was looming and her odds of success were decreasing every day. It wasn't the money—his acting career had taken off. It was that the cycles were so hard on both of them—between the hormones and the shots, she was physically and emotionally strung out. No matter how hard she tried to be optimistic, each failed cycle plunged her deeper into depression. Donny was losing patience with the emotional roller coaster. They had agreed to investigate adoption, and it wasn't as though she had anything against it. After all, she herself was adopted and adored her parents and her sister. But she wanted to know what it was like to have a biological connection to another human being. That was why having her own child was so important to her. She was all set to explain it to him again, to promise she'd stay steady this time, that she wouldn't allow herself to get so emotionally invested. But she never got the chance. Instead he'd walked in that night, steered her into the kitchen, and sat her down. He wouldn't meet her eyes.

"What's going on?"

"I don't know how to tell you this." He'd put his head in his hands and grown quiet.

"You're scaring me, Donny. What is it?"

He blew out a breath then spoke in a rush. "I can't do this

anymore. Neither of us has been happy in a while. It's become all about having a child. I need a break."

She shot up from her chair. "What? What are you talking about? I know it's been hard, but we love each other. We'll get through this. Donny, please!"

He shook his head and his eyes filled. "I'm sorry, I really am. But . . . it's Sasha. She's pregnant."

"What does that have . . ." Then it dawned on her. "Wait. It's yours?"

He nodded.

She felt as though she'd been punched in the gut. This couldn't be happening. "How could you?" A grief so profound filled her that she couldn't breathe. "How long has this been going on?"

"I never meant for it to happen. We both feel terrible, but"—he shrugged—"we're going to be a family."

Those six words were what really knocked the wind from her. He and Sasha: a family. That was all she had ever wanted, and now he was leaving her to make it happen with another woman. A woman she had trusted with her most intimate secrets and fears. In that moment, Iris wanted to die.

She heard the door chime, and realized her husband was home. She wiped the tears from her face and went to greet him, smiling as he walked toward her and pulled her into a long hug. Alan was so different from Donny. Good-looking in a wholesome, outdoorsy way, his brown hair always a little bit shaggy, his brown eyes warm and intelligent. He understood her better than Donny ever had, and she felt more at ease with him than she'd ever felt with anyone—even her own sister.

He kissed her and pulled back to look at her.

"You've been crying. You okay?"

"Yeah, just . . . seeing them brought up some old stuff."

"You wanna talk about it?"

"Nope. What I want is to welcome my husband home properly. Why don't you go get unpacked and I'll bring up a bottle of wine?" She put a hand on his arm. "But first, go check on Molly. She had another nightmare and was asking for you. She's asleep now, but make sure she doesn't need you before you come to bed."

He smiled at her. "Will do. And cookie, just for the record, any man who would let you go is a damn fool, and not worth another thought."

# Chapter Four
## Sasha

It was the week from hell. Donny was filming fourteen hours a day and Angela was sick, so Sasha had had to call Household Staffing for a temporary nanny. When she got home from back-to-back appointments at the clinic, Bailey wanted Sasha to play with her, have dinner with her, and read to her before bed—the temp wasn't cutting it. Normally, Sasha would be relaxing after a tiring day at work and enjoying a glass of wine with Donny while Angela went through the motions of childcare.

Now she closed the door and turned to face Bailey once Margaret, interim nanny, had left. "Did you have a good time with Margaret after school?" she asked.

"Yes. She's nice. We played some games."

"Oh, really?" Sasha said distractedly, sighing as she took off her cashmere jacket and threw it over the back of a chair.

"And Mommy, guess what? I got to read to the class and Ms. Kelly gave me a gold star. She said I'm a really good reader."

"Mm-hmm. That's nice," Sasha said, pulling out her iPhone to see if she had any messages from Donny.

Bailey ran from the room and came back holding a large piece of paper. "Look what I painted," she said, her voice loud with excitement. "I made the flowers purple and yellow 'cause they're your favorite flower colors. Do you like it?"

*Why are children so loud?* Sasha wondered for the thousandth time. She wanted to put her hands over her ears, but instead smiled and looked at the picture Bailey had painted. "It's very nice, Bailey."

"It's a present for you. You can hang it up if you want. Then you can see the pretty flowers every day!"

Sasha took the picture from her. "Yes." She laid it on the kitchen counter. "I'll hang it up later."

"Can we have pizza for dinner tonight?" Bailey was dancing around her now. The child just never stood still.

"Let's go see what Marcel made." Sasha had told the cook that Donny wouldn't be home for dinner at all this week, which meant the meals could be vegetarian, her preference.

"It's probably yucky. Like last night," Bailey complained as she followed her mother into the kitchen.

"Oh, stop it. Let's take a look," Sasha said, and raised the lid of the pot. "Mmm. Spinach and lentils. Smells delicious."

"Yuck. Can't we have pizza? Please, please?" Bailey pleaded.

Sasha hated that whiny voice. "Fine. If you want to eat pizza and get fat, go for it."

Bailey's eyes filled with tears, and she looked down at the floor, her lip trembling. Sasha felt a twinge of guilt, but it was momentary. How was her daughter going to learn what to eat and what not to eat if Sasha didn't guide her?

"How about I make you an open-faced grilled cheese on gluten free bread? I can add a bit of tomato sauce, and it'll be just like pizza. But healthier. What do you say?"

"I'm not hungry," Bailey said, and walked away mumbling under her breath.

Sasha thought she heard her say, "I don't like you," but she couldn't be sure. She shrugged. Kids said that all the time, she knew, and one day Bailey would thank her for keeping her on the straight and narrow where food was concerned. She spooned the lentils and spinach onto a plate, poured herself a glass of sparkling water, and sat at the kitchen island, ruminating. When she'd decided to get pregnant, Sasha didn't think through everything that went into raising a child. Movies and books romanticized it, never showing the daily monotony, the constant demands, the tantrums and neediness. Children were greedy and self-centered little creatures who always wanted to be the center of attention. Kind of like movie stars.

She thought of one of her patients, whose in vitro procedure had resulted in a pregnancy of triplets. When Sasha had read the sonogram, she thanked God for small miracles. She didn't know what she'd do if she were pregnant with triplets. Imagine having three Baileys to deal with. In moments like that, she wondered why she hadn't chosen a different specialty. But it was lucrative being a reproductive endocrinologist, and she enjoyed the challenge of working around a couple's presenting infertility issues and finding a solution to make them a family. It was like solving a puzzle. When she was successful, she was the object of their adoration, almost godlike, and their appreciation knew no bounds. Every year they'd send her pictures of their kids, and the walls of her clinic were filled with the photographs of the children her efforts had made possible.

She finished her meal in peace, and despite Bailey saying she wasn't hungry, Sasha fixed the sandwich for her and took it into the den where her daughter sat on the sofa reading a book. Sasha sat down next to her, feeling bad about their earlier harsh exchange. She should have been more patient, but it was so difficult when she came home needing peace and quiet and was instead met with the stresses of motherhood. It was especially tough when Donny was working long hours, and everything was left to her. And, well, the nanny too, of course.

"Here, honey." Sasha set the tray of food on the coffee table. "Have something to eat."

Bailey didn't acknowledge Sasha, her gaze remaining focused on the book.

Sasha rolled her eyes. "Bailey, come on now. I know you're hungry."

Bailey continued to ignore her.

"Fine. Suit yourself." Sasha rose in a huff. As she pivoted to leave the room, Donny came striding in.

"Donny!" Sasha said, surprised that he was home so early.

Before she reached him, Bailey flew past her and threw her arms around her father's waist.

"Daddy, you're home."

"Hey, sunshine," he said, sweeping Bailey up in his arms and kissing her. "How was your day?" Taking her hand, he walked with her to Sasha and gave her a quick peck on the lips.

"Daddy?" Bailey looked up at him and pulled on his hand to drag him away from Sasha. "I'm so hungry. Can't we get some pizza for dinner?"

Donny looked at his watch. "You haven't had dinner yet?"

"No." Bailey gave him a beseeching look.

He frowned at Sasha. "It's eight o'clock. How come she hasn't eaten?"

Sasha burned with anger. Why was the child always trying to drive a wedge between them? "She refused to eat what Marcel made. So I made her something else," she said, pointing to the sandwich on the tray, "and she refused to even look at it." Sasha glared at Bailey, who was leaning against Donny as if she were glued to him.

He knelt and ruffled Bailey's long brown hair. "Why don't you come to the kitchen with me, and we'll have dinner together. What do you say?

"I don't like spinach. Or lentils."

Donny laughed and stood up. "Me neither—no wonder you didn't eat. Spinach and lentils? I say we order pizza."

Bailey jumped up and down, clapping her hands. "Yay!"

Donny did this all the time—gave in to Bailey's every wish. And it drove Sasha crazy. She stormed from the room and climbed the elaborate curving staircase to their bedroom, slamming the door.

# Chapter Five
## Iris

Donny and Sasha would never deign to live in a house so completely average, but Iris loved the casual feel of her home. Its clean lines and manageable size, the backyard, pool, and patio—it all suited her just fine. She covered the fruit salad and put it in the refrigerator. The salmon, marinating for the last hour, and the asparagus were ready to be grilled. As she left the kitchen and walked through the airy ranch house she and Alan bought when they'd married a year ago, she sighed in contentment. She went outside and sat in one of the lounge chairs by the pool. Alan and Molly had gone to the beach, a jaunt they would normally have all done together, but Iris was on a strict editing deadline and had needed the day to finish. She expected them home any time now—her husband and stepdaughter. It still filled her with surprise. When Donny had left her bereft and heartbroken, Iris never would have believed that one day she'd be married to an incredibly wonderful man or that she would finally be a mother at the age of forty-four. She remembered that forty-fourth birthday and her girlfriends' insistence that she let them take her out for a night on the town to celebrate. She hadn't felt much like celebrating, but she'd acquiesced. It turned out to be the night that changed her life.

After her birthday dinner at Firefly, three of her friends had taken Iris to La Cita Bar for drinks and some live music. The crowd was friendly, and a trio of men seated at the next table introduced themselves. Iris never would forget the feeling she had when Alan smiled at her and told her his name. There was something in his eyes that drew her in, something reassuring and uplifting. They wound up talking for the next hour while the others talked and joked around them. She still remembered their conversation that night almost word for word. "What kind of work do you do, Iris?" Alan had asked.

"I'm a freelance editor. Literary fiction."

Alan's face lit up. "I can't resist a woman who loves to read. Who are your favorite writers?"

"Oh, gosh, so many. I love Henry James and Sinclair Lewis. Ian McEwan, Toni Morrison, Alice Munro, Garcia Márquez, Ishiguro, Edith Wharton." She laughed. "I'm all over the map. You're a big reader?"

"Absolutely. Hemingway, Aldo Leopold, Paul Ehrlich. And others."

"Is it fair to guess that your work has something to do with environmental issues?" she asked, after hearing the names.

"Spot-on. I write and produce documentaries on the environment."

"Oh, of course. I've seen your work," she realized.

The conversation never lagged for a moment after that.

"And what is your favorite thing, Alan Thomas?" she asked after they exhausted talk of books and authors.

"My daughter and my work," he said without hesitation.

Iris felt deflated. "You're married?"

"I was. My wife died six months ago."

"Oh, I'm so sorry."

They sat together talking long after the others had left, and for the first time since her divorce, Iris felt the cloud of sorrow begin to lift. She did feel some trepidation in getting involved with him so soon after his wife had died, but he was persistent, and after dating for six months, they were married in a quiet ceremony at the courthouse.

She wanted nothing more than to be a mother to Molly, but the child was understandably resistant. She was five when tragedy took her mother from her, and although she needed a maternal figure in her life, she wasn't ready for anyone to step into Linda's shoes. Not that she was unkind to Iris—her sweet nature would never allow that. And the moment Iris had laid eyes on the adorable little girl, she had felt her heart melt. She understood that it would take time for Molly to accept her and open her heart fully, and she was willing to wait. She was determined to do her best to help Molly hold on to the memory of Linda by keeping photographs of her around the house and including her in their nighttime prayer. She'd already grown to love Molly and to think of her as her daughter, and she hoped that one day Molly would call her the one name she'd been yearning to hear for almost ten years: Mommy.

She heard the front door open and the sound of Alan and Molly's voices. "We're home," they called in unison.

Iris rose from the chair and hurried inside. "I missed you guys." She went up on tiptoes to give Alan a quick kiss and then pulled Molly into her arms. "Did you have fun, sweet pea?" she asked.

"We went swimming, and then we saw starfish in the aquarium. They were so pretty. And I went on three rides. And I got a chocolate ice cream cone." She looked down at the floor, quiet for a moment. "But I missed Mommy. She always went on the rides with me."

Iris had learned it was better to let those comments pass without answering. It only upset Molly more when Iris tried to dig into her feelings. "You went to the pier?" She looked at Alan. "Was it crowded?"

"Packed."

"I bet," Iris said. "You had a long day. Are you hungry for dinner?"

"We can wait a little. Right, Molly?"

"Yeah. Can I play a game on my iPad?"

"You can have a half hour of screen time. I'll put the timer on, okay?" Iris said.

"Okay," she said, running off to her room.

"Sounds like you had a good day together," Iris said.

"It was fun. Would have been more fun with you, though. Did you finish your work?"

"I did. How about a glass of wine before dinner?"

"Perfect," he said, going to the kitchen with her, uncorking a bottle of Cabernet and pouring two glasses.

"To us," he said, clinking his glass against hers.

"Let's go outside and sit." Iris wanted their conversation to be private. Once they'd settled on the patio, she spoke. "You know

Molly's been asking about a sleepover with Bailey for a while now. Well, I got a call today from Bailey's nanny, Angela, about it."

Alan looked taken aback. "What? The nanny called instead of Sasha?"

"Yes, but I'm just as happy not to have to deal with Sasha. Honestly, I wish the girls weren't such good friends. I hate the idea of having to deal with Sasha and Donny."

"I know."

"I mean, I guess I knew with Molly going to Beardsley it was possible that she'd end up in same class as Bailey. But what are the chances they'd become best friends?"

Alan rose and positioned himself at the bottom of Iris's lounge chair, putting his hand on her calf. "I'm sorry. I know this is difficult for you. It's just such a great school for Molly. Before Linda died, she and I agreed that we'd try a year at the public school and if Molly didn't thrive, we'd move her. Molly's a kid that gets lost in a big classroom."

She sighed. Hearing Linda's name always filled her with a sense of melancholy as well as a feeling of guilt that she was somehow usurping Linda's rightful role as Molly's mother. It didn't matter that it was illogical—she hadn't even met Alan until after Linda died—but Iris guessed it must be natural to feel that way. "Of course, I understand that. And I would never jeopardize Molly's education or dishonor your and Linda's wishes. We'll get through it. I just wish Molly had found a different best friend."

"Me too. Are you concerned about Molly spending the night at

Bailey's?"

"I don't know. The weird thing is that Angela didn't invite Molly there. She made it pretty clear that she'd be happy to have Bailey come *here* for the sleepover. I got the distinct impression that they'd rather we host. She even texted me a list of instructions, if you can believe that!"

Alan cocked an eyebrow. "Like what?"

Iris picked up her phone and went to the text. "Lights out by eight o'clock, no PG movies, make sure she brushes her teeth for two full minutes, no scary bedtime stories." She rolled her eyes. "It's a little insulting. I mean seriously, does Sasha think I'm an idiot?"

He rubbed his hand back and forth along her leg. "She sounds like a control freak. That says volumes more about her than you."

Iris scrolled down, scanning the long text. "Oh, I didn't even notice this. I was so annoyed I stopped reading. Bailey's allergic to strawberries and raspberries. Wouldn't you think she'd lead with that?"

"Well, that's one thing they don't need to worry about, since you're allergic too," Alan said.

# Chapter Six
## Sasha

Sasha checked her reflection one last time before heading downstairs, adjusting the diamond headband over the blond wig and striking a vampy pose. Perfect. She looked *just* like Daisy Buchanan. The school's annual fundraising gala was being held tonight at the Beverly Hilton, and the theme was famous literary figures. Sasha, the chair of the committee organizing the event, had first pick of character—everyone wanted to be Jay Gatsby and Daisy Buchanan, but Sasha knew that she and Donny were the perfect couple for the roles. Like Daisy, Sasha was charming and beautiful, even if the charm was sometimes a pretense. And Donny . . . well, Donny would give his eyeteeth to rise above being a television doctor and show his acting chops by tackling a complicated character like Jay Gatsby.

He was waiting for her at the bottom of the stairs, looking dashing in his white suit.

"You look marvelous, darling," he said, affecting an Oxford accent.

She smiled and straightened his bow tie. "Did Gerald bring the car around?"

"Yes, he's waiting outside."

Bailey came speeding into the hallway, a Popsicle in one hand, and ran up to Sasha, throwing her arms around her. "Mommy, you look so pretty. I love your purple dress!"

"Be careful. No sticky hands." She gently pushed Bailey away from her, and the child looked down at the floor, suddenly quiet. When Sasha saw the look on Donny's face, she softened her tone. "Sorry, sweetie, it's just that it's a costume party, and I don't have anything else to wear if this gets ruined." She gave her a bright smile. "Daddy and I are going to bid on the sleepover at the school. You can take three friends, so think about who you'd like to invite if we win, okay?"

Bailey jumped up and down. "I want to take Molly!"

Sasha suppressed a groan. Of course she'd want to bring Molly. Why couldn't her daughter make other friends? "All right then, we'll do our best to win it. But think of some other friends too, in case Molly can't come."

They would end up paying a pretty penny for the prize—all the kids wanted it—but they could afford it, so whatever, she decided. She'd make a big deal of passing on other items of interest to her so that they could justify paying an outrageous price for the sleepover. At least it would earn her points with Donny.

"Okay, go find Angela and get cleaned up. Love you." She gave Bailey a quick peck on the cheek, and they were on their way.

They arrived at the hotel amid a stream of other cars and limousines, and as they got into the elevator on their way to the Stardust Penthouse, they were joined by parents dressed as Rhett Butler and Scarlett O'Hara.

"Love your costumes," Sasha gushed.

"Thank you. Yours is great too, Daisy," the woman said,

smiling. "We just saw Paris and Helen of Troy in the lobby. This is such fun."

The penthouse had been set up earlier that day by the committee in charge and looked magnificent, with romantic canopies, soft candlelight at round tables, and groups of love seats forming cozy seating areas under the stars. Two bars were already busy serving drinks, and a jazz quartet played softly in the background. It had come together beautifully, and Sasha, pleased with herself, turned to Donny. "Should we go inside and take a look at the auction items?" She linked her arm in his.

"Let's do it. I'll buy whatever your heart desires, Daisy dear." He laughed, propelling her to the long rows of tables.

They took their time, bidding on items here and there and stopping to chat with friends as they made their rounds, but Sasha found herself distracted, on the lookout for Iris. Everyone had to submit their costume choice ahead of time to ensure there were no doubles, so Sasha knew Iris was coming as Elizabeth Bennet and her husband as Mr. Darcy. Leave it to Iris to identify with Lizzy—she probably fancied herself so much smarter than the rest of them, which was absurd, of course. It's not like Iris went through medical school. She didn't know why, but something about Iris always made her feel like she wasn't quite cultured enough, that she was missing something.

Sasha and Donny walked back outside to the terrace, and suddenly, Iris and Alan appeared. She had to admit that Iris looked beautiful in a floaty blue empire-line dress with a pearl pendant at her throat. Her hair was swept up, with wispy tendrils grazing her neck. Alan, in breeches and topcoat, had his arm firmly around her waist, and they looked for all the world that they'd just come from Pemberley. She peered at Donny to see if he'd noticed Iris, but he seemed oblivious. Still, it was aggravating that she had to run into her at every school function. When Donny had divorced Iris and married her, Sasha assumed that would be the last of her. After all, she and Donny had no children together, so there'd be no reason for them to remain in each other's lives. Sasha never dreamed that she'd have a stepdaughter at the same school as Bailey. It was infuriating.

"There's your ex over there," Sasha said to Donny. "She should have come as Little Orphan Annie."

"Be nice now." Donny put his arm around her. "Iris isn't an orphan. She was adopted."

Sasha waved her hand dismissively. "You go mingle while I go say hello to her."

After he'd walked away, Sasha moved toward them. "Hello, Iris, Alan. I hope you're enjoying yourselves."

"We are. Everything looks beautiful," Iris said, but Sasha could tell that her smile was forced.

"Yes, my committee worked tirelessly, and I think it shows. Jillian and Annette outdid themselves on the silent auction items." Sasha wanted to make sure Iris knew that well-known actresses like Jillian and Annette were part of her entourage.

"I guess it's lucky we have parents like them, or how would we get such incredible donations?" Alan said. It sounded like a dig to Sasha, but Alan's face betrayed nothing.

"Yes, well, as one of the hostesses tonight, I hope you enjoy yourselves. And be sure to bid on something." She flashed a smile and walked away, feeling superior once again. She ordered a coconut martini from the bar and went inside to find Donny, who was surrounded by a group of fan parents. One of the things she enjoyed most about being married to him was the excitement and adoration of people whenever they saw him, and Sasha basked in that recognition by association. She loved being the envied wife of heartthrob Donny McBride, and when they realized she was not only young and beautiful, but a doctor as well, she watched with satisfaction as their eyes opened even wider in wonder.

She pushed her way through the crowd around Donny and stood next to him, sipping her martini and chatting with everyone until it was time for the live auction. The bidding was lively and profitable, and finally the last item was up: the school sleepover for four students.

"The bidding starts at five thousand dollars," the auctioneer said. "Can I have five thousand?"

Sasha put her hand up.

"I have five thousand. Do I hear seven?"

Another parent put up a hand, and it went back and forth that way until the bid reached sixteen thousand dollars.

"Eighteen," Sasha called.

There was silence, and then a new voice called, "Twenty

thousand."

Sasha spun around to see who it was. Alan! What the hell? "Twenty-one," she called.

"Twenty-five," came Alan's rapid reply.

There was no way she was going to let Alan and Iris outbid her. "Forty! Thousand!"

There was an audible gasp from the crowd. "What the hell are you doing?" Donny whispered in her ear.

"This is for Bailey," she shot back, waiting to hear if Alan was going to counter. She turned and saw him shake his head no, then smiled as the auctioneer brought down the gavel and said "Sold."

And what was forty thousand dollars, anyway? Donny made that in one day. It was a small price to pay.

Now the dance music started, and she took Donny's hand in hers. They were one of the first couples on the dance floor, but soon they were joined by so many others that the space became crowded. Sasha pushed her body against his for the first slow dance, peering over his shoulder at Alan and Iris. They were wrapped in each other's arms, and Iris's eyes were closed, her head leaning against him, and Sasha was incensed at Iris's apparent happiness.

# Chapter Seven
## Iris

Iris watched as the black SUV, its windows opaque and dark, pulled into their circular driveway and came to a stop. The sticky issue of who would pick up Bailey had been solved with Sasha's phone call yesterday.

"I've called the school and given them permission to release Bailey to our driver after school tomorrow. He'll bring her to your house."

"Wouldn't it be easier if Bailey just comes with me when I pick up Molly?"

There was an exasperated sigh on the other end of the line. "I'd feel better if she were in our vehicle with a driver I trust." She hurried on. "I mean, not that I'm saying you're a bad driver, but, well, I really don't know that, do I?"

Iris shook her head as she listened. "Sure, that's fine. Is it all right for Bailey to go in the pool? I always stay with Molly when she's swimming."

"Yes, that's no problem."

"Good. I suppose your driver will pick her up on Saturday as well. What time would you like her home?"

"We have a party Saturday night, so it doesn't matter. Any time that's convenient for you is fine. You've probably read that Donny has been nominated for an Emmy in the best actor category. The party's in his honor, so I'm not sure what time we'll be home, but of course Bailey's nanny will be here for her."

Now, instead of pulling the car into the garage, Iris turned off the engine and got out, opening the back door for Molly, who ran to the big SUV.

"Hello." Iris nodded at the driver as he opened Bailey's door and grabbed her suitcase from the back.

"Bailey!" Molly squealed, grabbing her friend's hand. "Hurry up. Come on."

The two girls scampered off, waiting at the front door for Iris to come up the walk.

"Okay, ladies," she said brightly as she punched in the code and swung the door open, "do you want to change out of your uniforms before you have a snack?"

"Can we put our bathing suits on?" Molly asked.

"Of course." Iris closed her hand around the handle of Bailey's suitcase.

"I can get that, Mrs. Thomas," Bailey said. "It just rolls."

"Okay. You girls get changed, and I'll have your snacks ready in a jiffy."

The sounds of little girls' chatter and laughter brought back memories of times with her sister when they were young. Adopted as a baby, Iris had had a happy childhood, and she and Violet were as close as any blood sisters might have been. But later on, all attempts by Iris to find her biological parents had been met with frustration and dead ends.

When Molly and Bailey returned to the kitchen, they each took a seat at the breakfast bar, and Iris put a plate of fruit and muffins in front of them.

Bailey took a chocolate chip muffin and bit into it. "Did you make these?" she asked Iris.

Molly answered before Iris could. "We made them together. Iris is a good cooker."

Iris smiled. "Do you like them?"

Bailey nodded. "I wish I knew how to bake."

"Well, next time you come over, we can do that."

Bailey gave Iris an excited smile. "Really? What if I mess up the kitchen?"

Iris felt a stab in her heart. Sasha clearly didn't appreciate this sweet child. "Who cares? That's what paper towels and sponges are for."

When they finished their snacks, they scooted off the stools and walked to the back door and out to the pool.

Iris's attention was drawn to a mole with an unusual shape in the center of Bailey's back. She focused her gaze on it, wondering if she was seeing things. But no, it was exactly like the one on her own back. What a strange coincidence.

"Girls, sit in the chairs by the side of the pool and wait for me before going into the water. I'm going to change into my suit."

She hurried to her room and changed, but before leaving she grabbed a hand mirror and held it up against her bedroom mirror. Moving closer for a better look, Iris saw that it was not an exact match. But it was similar enough, she told herself as she returned to the pool where the girls were dutifully waiting on chairs.

"Lifeguard on duty," Iris said. "Hold on, before you go in, and let me get a picture of you two." She snapped a few with her cell phone. "Okay, go ahead in." She watched as they swam, taking pictures for a few minutes before clicking the Google search bar and typing, *Are moles hereditary?* The results weren't encouraging, with words like *seem to occur, a tendency*, and *inheritance pattern is not yet understood.* Nothing concrete either way.

Iris put down her phone and turned her attention to the girls splashing and laughing in the water, while Oscar paddled and barked with excitement. It was a joy to see Bailey carefree and happy, and Iris suddenly felt fiercely protective of the little girl with the strict, distant mother. Bailey not only had a friend in Molly; she now had a guardian in Iris. Iris was going to be there for Bailey, no matter what happened, and no matter what Sasha threw at her.

# Chapter Eight
## Sasha

Sasha was exhausted. She wasn't a miracle worker, yet sometimes patients expected just that. And the ones for whom her efforts failed were a drain on her patience. The worst were the actresses and other high-profile career women who'd put off trying until their late thirties, and then railed against her when she told them there was nothing more she could do for them. They accused her of depriving them of their *right* to procreate. They were achievement-oriented, used to getting what they wanted when they wanted it. Sasha felt like telling them that they should have done their research before waiting so long. Fertility began its decline in a woman's late twenties. It wasn't like getting Botox or plastic surgery, where you could fool the world into believing you were younger than you were. Mother Nature would not be tricked. And then there were the sad sacks—the ones who didn't blame Sasha but expected her to hold their hands while they cried over their lost dreams. Isn't that what therapists were for? She was busy. She didn't have time to waste, but she did have a reputation to uphold, and so she sat, feigned empathy, and comforted them when what she really wanted to tell them was to get on with their lives.

She grudgingly admitted that Iris hadn't been like any of those women. She hadn't come to see Sasha with a sense of entitlement. In fact, she never would have ended up on Sasha's examining table at all if Donny hadn't persuaded her to switch doctors. Sasha had been consulting on Donny's show for a few weeks when one night the two of them went to grab a drink afterward. She'd known he was married, of course, but in this town, marriages were about as permanent as Botox. They were on their second glass of wine when he began to open up.

"It's so strange, you know, how life imitates art, or maybe the other way around."

She leaned in closer toward him. "What do you mean?"

"I'm playing this fertility doc and spouting all this advice on my show, and in the meantime, my wife and I are going through the same thing. And I have no words of comfort for her."

She gave him a concerned look. This was perfect—a way in. "Oh, I'm so sorry to hear that. Have you been trying for long?"

He nodded, taking another sip from his glass. "Four years." He blew out a breath. "We've run the gamut, and we're on our sixth IVF cycle. She'll be forty soon, and the doctor is telling us we're running out of time. He's done all kinds of tests, but it's unexplained infertility. It just doesn't take."

Sasha digested this information. Four years of fertility treatments was hell on a marriage. And if six cycles of IVF hadn't worked, it was unlikely the next one would be successful, especially with forty looming. "Has she been able to conceive at all? Any miscarriages?"

"No, which is another reason I'm not holding out too much hope." He sighed. "I always imagined a house full of kids. I know I'm blessed in so many ways, but sometimes I wonder what it's all for. Maybe it's selfish, but I think we all want to leave a legacy."

"Of course. It's perfectly natural. Have you considered using a surrogate?"

He shook his head. "Iris is adamant. She wants to carry the child."

Sasha wanted to roll her eyes. There were a lot of things that people wanted; that didn't mean they got them, she thought.

"Who are you seeing, if you don't mind my asking?"

"Dr. Brady over on Sunset."

"Well, as you know, this is my specialty. And not to brag, but they don't call me the miracle doctor for nothing. I'd be happy to see your wife. See if there's anything I might do differently."

He raised his eyebrows. "Really? You'd do that? I tried to get in last year, but you had a two-year waiting list."

She waved a hand. "It would be my pleasure. I'll get you both in this week."

"Wow, this is amazing. I can't thank you enough."

He leaned back in the bar stool and looked at her. "I'm sorry for making it all about me. What about you?" He glanced at her hand. "Are you married?"

"No. My work keeps me pretty busy. But hopefully the right man will come along, and we'll fill the house with kids. I've got the same dream." That was a lie, but she was rewarded with a look of approval. She had no desire to have kids, ever. But something about Donny made her willing to do whatever was necessary to make him hers. She'd felt it from the moment she'd laid eyes on him. Sasha reached out and squeezed his hand. "It's really not selfish, you know, wanting a legacy. It's a biological drive." She laughed. "The species would have ended if we didn't have this need, this consuming compulsion to procreate. People get desperate when they can't fulfill that need. It's what makes my work so rewarding. Helping couples become families."

"I'm so grateful that you're willing to take us on," he said. "To be honest, I feel hopeful for the first time in a long time."

She smiled at him. There was likely nothing more that she could do for them. Brady was a top man in the field. But she did want to get a look at Iris—check out the competition. Sasha knew from her experience as a doctor that sex for a couple going through fertility treatments became a chore. Sex on demand driven by an ovulation cycle took all the appeal out of it, and the men began to feel like nothing more than sperm donors. Donny was vulnerable. Any attention he got from an attractive woman would be welcome, and Sasha was more than willing to give it to him. Besides, Iris had had her chance. The fact that she wasn't willing to exhaust every channel to make him a father showed her lack of commitment to him. It was selfish. Plenty of women used surrogates. But first things first. She had to meet her, to win over her trust. In the meantime, she and Donny would be working late plenty of nights. Donny deserved to be a father, and Sasha would be happy to make him one.

# Chapter Nine
## Iris

"When can I have another playdate with Bailey? You promised we could do it soon. How many days since she came here?" Molly put her spoon down and gave Iris a petulant look.

"I'm waiting for her nanny to call me back."

Molly's eyes filled with tears. "Do you think Bailey doesn't like me anymore?"

Iris reached out and tucked a curl behind Molly's ear. "Of course not. Her nanny must have forgotten. I'll make sure I talk to her today." Iris had, in fact, already left two messages for Angela. Sasha had probably decreed a moratorium on any further get-togethers, she thought. She obviously cared more about her own feelings than her daughter's, and it burned Iris up. The friendship between Molly and Bailey wasn't going to fade, and the sooner Sasha realized that, the better. As much as she dreaded it, she was going to have to confront Sasha.

It was hard to believe that Sasha had once been someone that Iris admired and looked up to. Even more than Donny, the person Iris had most leaned on during her battle with infertility had been her doctor. She'd had a great relationship with Dr. Brady, but when Donny came to her about switching, she was ready to do anything that might give her new hope. Sasha Everett, MD, was known as the miracle doctor among the Southern California elite. Iris still remembered the first time she laid eyes on her. She and Donny had been ushered into Sasha's office, and when she greeted them, Iris was momentarily taken aback by how stunning the doctor was. Her silky black hair was cut in a stylish bob, and her eyes were so blue almost startling. Living so near Hollywood, Iris was used to beautiful women, but she hadn't expected the doctor to look like she'd just stepped off a movie set.

"So nice to meet you, Iris. Can I get you something to drink?"

"Um, no, I'm good, thanks," she'd answered. She'd never been offered a beverage at a doctor's appointment before.

"Thank you for having your records sent. I've gone over them, and I'd like to run a few more tests. A thyroid panel, first, since it's been a few years since Dr. Brady ran one."

They spoke for the next hour, with Sasha going over everything in meticulous detail, despite her packed schedule. By the time they left, Iris felt like she couldn't be in better hands.

"Thank you, Donny." She kissed him when they got to their car. "I really appreciate your getting us in to see her. Clearly she lives up to her reputation."

But when she'd gone through three more IVF cycles with no pregnancy, even Sasha had told them it was time to give up. Of course, Iris had no idea at the time that Sasha and Donny were already sleeping together. Then he came home and dropped the bombshell. He was going to start a family with the woman who was supposed to make *them* a family. The woman she had trusted with all her fears and disappointments. Her cheeks burned with humiliation as she thought of everything she'd shared with Sasha. She'd put all her hope in her, cried over failed cycles in her office, confided her marital struggles. Sasha had seen her at her most vulnerable, spread-eagle on the examination table. Dr. Sasha Everett, baby doctor to the stars. Her husband's mistress.

She had to know how long it had been going on. Before he left, she'd grabbed him and asked, "Were you screwing her when you persuaded me to switch doctors and go to her? What kind of a sick person does that?"

"No, no. Of course not! I really thought she could help us. I never meant for it to happen. We were spending a lot of nights together when she was helping me with the show. You've been so depressed, and I was lonely."

She'd lost it then, started screaming and actually threw a glass at him, which narrowly missed him. "Don't you dare blame me for this. I'll report her. It's unethical. I'll have her license revoked!"

But of course she never did. Sasha hadn't seduced *her*, after all. And she wasn't about to subject herself to more embarrassment by making a huge deal of it. It was bad enough that everyone would find out that her husband had left her for their fertility doctor—a beautiful younger woman who'd been able to give him a child when his pathetic infertile wife couldn't. Iris had left town for a while, gone to her parents' house in Portland just to get away. She hadn't wanted to risk running into Sasha, her belly swelling, when it should have been Iris carrying Donny's baby.

# Chapter Ten
## Sasha

Sasha's head was pounding. She'd had too much vodka at Donny's wrap party last night. She meant to pace herself, but when he disappeared for an hour with one of his female costars, she downed two more martinis to calm herself before he finally came back. Now, he was still sleeping, and she glanced over, still annoyed, and decided that they'd have a nice long talk this morning. But first, coffee. She sat up, and before her feet hit the floor, Bailey came running in.

"Mommy, Mommy! Can we make pancakes for breakfast?"

Where was Angela? She knew better than to let the child come running into their bedroom like a banshee.

Sasha massaged her temples as she sat on the edge of the bed. "Go ask Angela. Mommy's still waking up."

"But I want you to make them. Molly's mommy let us help her. We made all kinds of cool shapes. She even has a Mickey Mouse one."

"Molly's *stepmother*," she corrected her daughter.

"Please, Mommy! I want to cook."

"Bailey! I told you to go find Angela. Mommy has a headache. We don't have any shapes to make them."

Bailey stared at her, her lower lip pouting. "You're no fun!" she said, and ran from the room.

Donny stirred and pushed the blanket back. "What was that all about?"

"I told you it wasn't a good idea to let Bailey spend so much time with Molly." She stood up and marched to the bathroom, downing two Advil and chasing them with the can of Diet Coke on the counter. Mickey Mouse pancakes. Ridiculous. Sasha was busy. She didn't have time to spend on such frivolous ventures like shopping for pancakes molds! She was still peevish after showering when she met Donny out on the deck for their Sunday morning coffee-and-paper ritual.

"I'm still pissed at you, you know," she said as she sat down next to him and poured herself a cup from the carafe Marcel had set on the table.

He gave her a sheepish grin. "I love it when you're jealous."

She arched an eyebrow. "It's bad enough that I have to watch you do those love scenes with Darby, I don't appreciate the two of going off alone and leaving me to fend for myself with your cast mates." Although she wouldn't admit it to him, she actually loved hanging out with his costars. They were young and gorgeous and the crème de la crème. But still, he should be at her side, letting them all see how much he adored her.

"I'm sorry, babe. She's going through a rough time with her divorce and needed some advice. She knew I'd been through it."

Sasha didn't like the sound of that. Too many marriages had been blown apart by some poor woman crying on the man's shoulder. "Still, it didn't look good. You know how this town is, rumors get started so easily. If I see something in the tabloids about the two of you, you're really in for it."

He leaned over and kissed her. "I only have eyes for you."

"Speaking of divorces, your ex-wife is on my last nerve."

"Oh?"

"Bailey can't stop going on and on about how much more fun Molly's house is than ours. Iris let them help her cook breakfast, they did finger painting, all sorts of crafty things. I mean, it's fine if that's how Iris wants to spend her time, she doesn't have a demanding career. But I can't do everything with her."

Donny chuckled. "I can just picture you flipping out as they run around with paint on their hands. You'd have a stroke."

Her mouth dropped open. "Are you comparing me unfavorably to *her*?"

"No, no. Of course not! You guys are night and day, that's all I'm saying. Your priorities are different."

"Hmph, well, I guess if being oblivious to a mess and keeping a beautiful house are different priorities, then you're right. Whatever, the point is I don't want Bailey over there anymore. She needs to make new friends."

"Come on, Sash. I thought we settled this. You can't choose Bailey's friends, and you know she doesn't always have the easiest time making them. She's not like you in that way. I don't want her to be unhappy."

Sasha slammed her coffee cup on the table and stood up. "Oh, but it's okay if *I'm* unhappy? Honestly, Donny, sometimes I think you love Bailey more than you love me."

She didn't miss the look of shock on his face, and she quickly realized her mistake. "I didn't mean it that way. Of course we both love her in a different way then we love each other. I just meant that you and I are forever. You know, psychologists are always saying you have to put your spouse before your children. One day Bailey will grow up and leave, and it'll just be the two of us."

He sighed. "I'm not putting her *before* you. Let's not overreact, okay? It's normal for a kid to be excited about what they did at a friend's house. Try not to take it personally just because it happens to be Iris."

She sat back down. "I guess you're right."

She heard the unmistakable sound of Bailey's footsteps running toward them. She crashed into Donny, throwing her arms around him.

"Morning, Daddy! Can we go swimming? I want to wear my new Ariel bathing suit."

Donny gave her a broad smile. "Sure thing, pumpkin. Let Mommy and me finish our coffee, and I'll come and get you soon."

She looked at Sasha. "Will you swim too, Mommy?"

"We'll see. I'll sit by and watch you and Daddy."

"But you don't watch us. You just read. Why can't you play with me sometimes? Molly's mom always plays with us."

"Molly's *stepmother* doesn't have a big important job like Mommy does."

Bailey put her hands on her hips. "Yes, she does. She fixes books. Books are important."

Sasha gave Donny a withering look, then turned back to her daughter. "Yes, of course they are. But Mommy helps to make babies. That's more important."

56

# MISCONCEPTION

Before Bailey could answer, Donny stood and went over to her. "You know what? I think it's time for that swim now." Taking her hand, they walked back inside and left Sasha alone and seething.

# Chapter Eleven
## Iris

As soon as she had the chance, Iris cornered Sasha to find out whether she was intentionally avoiding setting up more playdates for the girls. It was after their monthly PTA meeting, and Sasha gave her a look of surprise.

"I don't know what you're talking about. We agreed that the girls can be friends." She reached into her Prada purse, pulled out a thick ivory business card, and held it out to her. "My nanny's number. Take it up with her." Iris didn't reach for the card.

"I've got Angela's number, thank you. She hasn't returned my calls all week."

Sasha emitted a heavy sigh, then rolled her eyes. "Good help is so hard to find these days. I'll speak with her about it."

Since then, the girls had at least two playdates a week, alternating between both homes. Iris was careful not to ask Molly too much about her time at Sasha's—she didn't want to make her stepdaughter uncomfortable or for Alan to think she was pumping her for information.

Three weeks after the confrontation, Iris was picking them both up from school—apparently Sasha now believed her a safe enough driver to allow her the privilege. She pulled up to the pickup line and waited. They were holding hands and smiling as they skipped to the car, their conversation rapid-fire.

"Hi! Can we get ice cream on the way? You promised last time that we could," Molly reminded her.

"Absolutely! I thought we'd go to Baskin-Robbins and grab a bunch of different flavors."

"Yes!" the girls said in unison.

Then Iris glanced in the rearview mirror and noticed Bailey whisper something to Molly.

"No, silly! You won't get fat from a little ice cream," Molly said, and Bailey's cheeks turned pink. "Right, Iris?"

"Of course not," she answered. "Molly and I are ice cream fanatics."

What was that all about? Iris thought. Just like Molly, Bailey was fit and trim. And she was only seven—why was she worried about her weight?

After they picked up the ice cream and got back to the house, Iris opened the containers and put out bowls, spoons, and toppings.

"Mol, I know you like chocolate. I'm having some of the mint chocolate chip. What would you like, Bailey?

"Mint chocolate chip is my favorite too!"

She fixed all the bowls, and the three of them sat around the table. Oscar ran up to Bailey, tail wagging furiously. She squealed with delight as she showered his head with kisses.

"You're so lucky you have a dog!"

"Iris got him as a present for me. Why don't you get one?" Molly said.

Bailey shook her head. "Mommy says dogs are filthy animals

that make your house dirty." She looked up at Iris with wide eyes. "I'm sorry, Mrs. Thomas! I don't think that, and your house isn't dirty!"

Iris laughed. Bailey was such a sweetheart. "No need to apologize, honey! I know that's not what you meant." She could only imagine what this poor child had to endure at the hands of Sasha.

"So, anything interesting happen at school today?" Iris asked.

"We got to pick our books," Bailey said, a huge smile spreading across her face. "Ms. Kelly told me the one I picked was too hard, but I read her the first page and she saw I could do it, so she had to let me."

"Good for you," Iris said. "No one should tell you which books are too hard. You know what you can handle." She needed to have a word with the teacher, she thought, annoyed. It was obvious that Donny and Sasha weren't paying enough attention to Bailey's educational needs. "What book was it?"

"The Mystery at Lilac Inn,"

"Oh, I *love* Nancy Drew books. I have the whole set. You're welcome to borrow any of them if you'd like."

"Thank you!" Bailey said. As she finished eating, she pushed her bowl aside and leaned back in her chair, twirling a strand of hair around her finger. Iris watched her, mesmerized. She had noticed Bailey doing it before. It was a habit that Iris herself had as a little girl. She forced her gaze away and turned to Molly.

"What about you, Mol? What book did you pick?" Iris asked.

"Amelia Bedelia Means Business," she answered.

"Of course!" Iris knew those were Molly's favorites.

"Books are the best," Bailey said.

"I couldn't agree more," Iris said.

They finished their ice cream, and Bailey brought her dish to the sink, then turned to Iris. "Can I help you clean up?"

She had to give Sasha credit for one thing; her daughter was extremely well-mannered. Of course, that could be more Angela than Sasha, she thought.

"Thanks, sweetie, but I've got it. Do you girls want to go swimming, or do you want to go to Molly's room and play?"

"Play," they both said and sailed out of the kitchen together with Oscar at their heels. After Iris finished in the kitchen, she decided to go to her home office and do some editing while the girls played. As she was walking past Molly's bedroom, she overheard Bailey.

"My mom told me that your mom and my dad used to be married."

"My mom wasn't married before," Molly answered. "Wait, you mean Iris?"

"Yeah. Sorry, I keep forgetting she's not your real mom," Bailey said. "Anyway, that kind of makes us sisters, right? And it sorta makes her my stepmom too."

Iris could hear the smile in Molly's voice when she answered. "Yes! I always wanted a sister." The two girls were giggling then, and Iris walked away, a sense of sadness filling her. Would there ever come a day when Molly would think of her as more than just her daddy's new wife? And sweet Bailey, it seemed, needed a mother as much as Molly did. From what she'd gleaned over the weeks Bailey had been coming over, Sasha barely had the time of day for her daughter. It incensed Iris—Sasha had everything, but she didn't appreciate it. As Iris walked away, she allowed herself a moment to fantasize that the girls actually were sisters and that she was their mother—not their stepmother. She imagined watching them grow from little girls into young ladies, and then fine young women, with her at the helm guiding their steps. She'd never pawn their upbringing off on a nanny or be more worried about having a clean house than happy children. It was all Iris had ever wanted—to have a family of her own. Growing up in a family where everyone looked alike except for her, she'd daydream about what it would be like when she could finally look at another human being and see something of herself reflected back. As close as she was to her sister and her adoptive parents, there was a part of her that felt adrift and unmoored, like a puzzle missing its central pieces. Infertility was hard enough to bear, but on top of it, she had no biological connection to anyone. Hers was a closed adoption, and despite her family's willingness to help her find her birth parents, she was unsuccessful. Even when she'd completed an ancestry DNA kit, no confirmed matches had been found. She would have to accept her fate—she'd never know the feeling of a blood connection to another person. She could daydream all she wanted, but the chance to have a child of her own was gone. But no matter how hard she tried, her deep yearning for a mother-child bond had only grown over the years, and the void sometimes felt so vast she worried that one day she might disappear into it entirely.

Alan was working late, and after Bailey was picked up, Iris finally got Molly down. She sat with her laptop and navigated to Facebook. Typing in Sasha's name, she found her profile right away and clicked on it. The profile was set to public, and Iris scrolled through her self-aggrandizing posts with disgust. She looked red-carpet ready in every shot and labeled them with obnoxious captions like *Home sweet humble home* in front of their Malibu mansion, or *Hands off girls, he's all mine* under a picture of Donny and her on their beach, Donny in board shorts and Sasha in a skimpy bikini showcasing her toned body. Clicking on the photos icon, she found what she was looking for: pictures of Bailey from infancy to now. She hovered over a picture of Bailey when she was a toddler and downloaded it, then enlarged it, and pulled out an old photo album from the bookshelf. She flipped through the pages until she found the ones of her as a young child and took one picture out. Holding it up to the computer, she compared the two. Her heart began to beat faster. In both photos, they were posed in an identical fashion, with both hands curled into fists under their chin. It was uncanny. It had to mean something. She thought of their other similarities—both avid readers who loved Nancy Drew books; both preferred mint chocolate chip ice cream, which was a unique flavor; the allergy to berries; certain mannerisms. Then there was the mole. And now this.

"Hey."

She jumped and spun around. "Alan. I didn't hear you come in."

"What are you doing?" He leaned over to look at the photos, then noticed the photo on the screen.

"Iris, what's going on?"

"Look at these two pictures. Do you see the resemblance between Bailey and me? It's almost like looking at the same person. We're posed exactly the same, our hair . . ."

His mouth dropped open. "What . . . well, that's a common pose photographers use for kids. They may be a little similar, but still. I don't understand. Why are you looking at pictures of Bailey anyway?"

"I went to Sasha's Facebook. Bailey has mannerisms that remind me of my younger self. You can't tell me you haven't noticed that she's a lot like me, every time she's here, I see more and more."

Concern filled his face. "Iris, what are you implying?"

"Well, come on, mistakes happen in fertility clinics. We've all heard stories of things like that."

He blew out a breath. "I'm assuming 'mistakes' only happen when two women are going through treatment at the same time. But honey, Sasha and Donny had an affair. Bailey is her child. You must see that. Maybe it's not a good idea for you to spend so much time around Bailey."

She bit down her frustration. She shouldn't have said anything to him. She needed to do more research. Alan was nothing if not logical and analytical—she was wasting her time trying to convince him. "Of course you're right. I'm just unsettled by having Donny and Sasha back in my life again." She waved a hand. "It was a silly thought.

Go on and grab dinner, I kept it warm for you. I'll be right out."

He seemed unconvinced as he glanced again at the photos and then at her. "Okay."

After he left, she put the photos in her desk drawer, and scrolled through the rest of the pictures on Facebook. She didn't know how Sasha had done it, but she was sure: Sasha had stolen her child.

66

# Chapter Twelve
## Sasha

As much as Sasha disapproved of Bailey spending so much time at Molly's, she had to admit that it was glorious to have the house to herself on the weekends she was there. No Angela underfoot chasing a bored Bailey while Sasha tried to have a relaxing Saturday. No waking up early on Sunday with Bailey demanding Donny's attention. This morning, she moved closer to Donny, pressing her body against his until he began to rouse and respond to her caresses.

"Good morning," he whispered, flipping around to face her and put his arms around her. "This is nice."

It had been almost two weeks since they'd last made love, and Sasha needed to fix that. Usually, she was vigilant about keeping him satisfied—after all, there were plenty of women who'd love the chance—but lately she'd been too stressed to make the effort. He was a good lover, thoughtful and energetic, but after almost eight years together, the excitement was gone. Sasha was all about the chase, and she already had Donny firmly in her grip. But as her mother had always reminded her, if you don't pay attention to your man, someone else will. So she pretended it was years ago, back when she'd set her sights on him and went to extraordinary measures to entice him away from his wife. Pushing him down, she straddled him and put her lips on his, teasing him with her tongue. She'd already brushed her teeth and gargled. He hadn't, but that was okay; she wasn't going to be up here for long.

"Lie back and relax, lover boy," she said as she slid down. She knew most wives didn't bother with this anymore, but she wasn't stupid. Men loved it, and it was a small price to pay to ensure that her husband wasn't tempted to look elsewhere. When she'd finished, she curled up next to him, her head on his chest, and closed her eyes.

"I love you, babe," he whispered as he drifted back to sleep.

They were up and showered a few hours later, on their way to brunch at Perch. Donny was in a good mood, naturally, and couldn't stop smiling at her all morning. He was a regular there, and they were seated immediately despite the line of waiting diners. She loved the view from the rooftop at Perch. Sitting up here and surveying Los Angeles, she always felt as though she'd finally arrived. It was a gorgeous day, sun shining brightly with just enough of a breeze to cool the heat of the sun.

"Bellinis or mimosas?" Donny asked.

"Bellinis. But tell them to make it with Dom," she said, looking around to see who was around.

"Of course. The usual for brunch?"

Donny ordered them the fruit plate and avocado toast. When their drinks arrived, he raised his glass to Sasha.

"To my sexy wife." He grinned at her.

"Right back atcha," she said and took a long sip. She sat up straight and smoothed her hair as Ian Johns, Hollywood's newest heartthrob, stopped at their table. Sasha was struck every time she saw him at how much bluer his eyes were in person than they looked on the big screen. He was being touted as the next Paul Newman.

"Hey, Donny, Sasha. Good to see you."

"Ian, you're looking well. Would you like to join us?" Donny asked.

He looked over his shoulder. "Meeting someone, actually. New gal pal." He winked at Donny, and Sasha wondered who the lucky girl was. They made small talk for a few minutes until a stunning redhead joined him. It took Sasha a moment to recognize her, but when she did, her blood ran cold. What the hell was Margo Simmons doing in LA? As Ian began to make introductions, Margo cocked her head at Sasha. "Susan? Is that you?"

Both Donny and Ian turned to look at her. "Susan?"

Sasha laughed. "I go by Sasha now. Good to see you, Margo— what a small world. How long have you been in town?" She glued a smile on her face and willed herself to stay calm.

"How do you two know each other?" Ian asked.

Margo put a hand on his arm possessively. "Susan . . . I mean Sasha . . . and I grew up together in Dalton. Course, Sasha was always eager to get out of Georgia. I mean, you'd hardly know she was from the South."

Margo's thick southern accent grated on Sasha's nerves. Sasha left everything about her hometown behind her when she was accepted to Columbia for undergrad and then medical school. Elocution lessons had taken care of her accent, and studying the other girls in her dorm had helped her with the rest. By the time she'd climbed her way to the top of the food chain in California, no one would ever guess at her humble beginnings.

"Well, now you have to join us," Donny said. "I want to hear all about Sasha's younger days." He looked at her. "I knew she was born in Georgia, but I thought she'd spent most of her childhood in New York?" He gave Sasha a questioning look.

"You got me," she said. "I guess after going to college and medical school there, I think of it as home. As I've told you, Donny, my childhood wasn't the happiest." She tried to look forlorn in the hopes he'd drop it.

Ian looked embarrassed. "We're meeting some friends, so we can't stay for long, but one drink should be okay," he said, making no reference to Sasha's comment about her childhood.

They sat down, and Sasha wanted to scream.

"Well, I can't believe you went to medical school like you always wanted! Good for you," Margo said.

"Oh, yes, Dr. Sasha Everett is Hollywood's preeminent fertility doctor—or, to be more clinically correct, a reproductive endocrinologist. She has a two-year waiting list. I'm so proud of her." Donny beamed.

Margo looked impressed. "Well, that does sound big-time. Wow. Good for you."

"What brings you to the Golden State?" Sasha asked.

"A part, what else? I finally decided to pursue my passion for acting, and I landed a role in Ian's new movie. It's how we met." At this, Ian leaned over and kissed her. Sasha wanted to vomit.

"So how long have you and Donny been married?"

70

"Almost eight years now."

"And we have a darling seven-year-old daughter," Donny said.

Margo's eyes widened, and she looked at Sasha. "A daughter? I thought you—"

Sasha groaned. "I don't feel well all of a sudden. Margo, would you come with me to the ladies'?"

When they got to the bathroom, Margo put a hand on her arm. "Are you okay?"

Sasha nodded. "I needed to get you alone." She grabbed Margo's hands in hers. "I know we lost touch, but we're still friends, right?"

Margo nodded. "Of course."

"I need your discretion. Donny doesn't know about . . . you know. Only you know what I went through after that reckless night. It's taken me years to come to terms with it and find a way to make the life I want. Please, not a word to Ian. Not a word to anyone."

Margo's eyes filled. "I'm sorry, Susan. You don't know how much I regret that night. Of course your secret's safe with me. But how . . ."

Sasha shook her head. "No questions. Just leave it. Promise me."

Margo nodded. "I promise. I won't let you down again."

# Chapter Thirteen
## Iris

Iris finished mixing the batter for the chocolate chip pancakes just as the girls woke up. Saturday night sleepovers were now a regular event and always included making their own pizza—one girl on each side of Iris on their step stools, where they concocted all sorts of pies with toppings ranging from pineapple to pureed potato. Bailey was always especially excited and loved helping Iris with everything. It was clear that she was starved for attention. Both the girls preferred sleepovers at Iris and Alan's house because, according to them, the bedtime ritual at Bailey's was much stricter. Sasha wanted lights out and no talking after eight p.m., while Iris and Alan turned a blind eye to their late-night chatting. She was sick and tired of Sasha's ridiculous rules. It infuriated her that Sasha had the privilege of raising Bailey when it was clear that she hardly spent any time with her. In fact, Iris was getting concerned about leaving Bailey in such a cold and unloving environment. There was a darkness in Sasha, Iris could sense it, and she was worried about what that might mean for Bailey. But what could she do about it? It wasn't like she could keep Bailey, as much as she wished she could. She had to be careful—she couldn't risk doing anything to jeopardize the time she did have with her. Iris loved these Saturday nights with the four of them snuggled on the sofa under a cozy throw blanket, eating popcorn as they enjoyed a movie. Even Molly had warmed up to Iris since Bailey had been spending so much time with them, seeming to appreciate Iris more now that Bailey was enchanted by her.

"Can we pour it into the molds?" Molly asked, running into the kitchen with Bailey close behind.

"Of course! And look, I got some new ones." Iris pointed to the counter.

"Oh, wow! Our initials! We need an *O* for Oscar," Bailey said.

Iris laughed. "No pancakes for Mr. Oscar, I'm afraid. But you can give him one of his dog bones."

Alan walked in and ruffled Molly's hair. "Good morning, princesses! Did everyone sleep well?"

"Mm-hmm," the girls both said, concentrating on making their pancakes.

Iris helped each girl flip her pancake, and they piled them on a plate as they were finished cooking. "Did you get an *A* for Daddy?" Molly asked.

Alan laughed. "Daddy is having yogurt this morning. I'll never be able to run if I gobble all those delicious chocolate chips."

"Did you see what Mommy Iris got us?" Molly asked.

Both Iris and Alan looked at Molly in surprise.

Bailey and Molly began to giggle. "It was Bailey's idea. It's okay if we call you that, right?" Molly asked.

Iris's eyes welled up. Molly was finally coming around, and it was all because of Bailey. On some level, Bailey must know the truth too! She could tell that Iris was her real mommy. "Of course. I would love that." She was thrilled, but she could see that Alan was

74

perplexed.

"It's a lovely idea, Mol," Alan said, then turned to Bailey. "What made you think of it?"

Bailey finished chewing the pancake in her mouth then answered. "Well, Iris used to be married to my daddy, so we like to pretend we're sisters. And I think Iris is a good mommy, but Molly doesn't want to hurt her real mommy's feelings. So, Mommy Iris is nice for both of us."

Alan gave Iris a look she couldn't quite discern. "I see," he said.

"Another thing that makes us sisters is we can both roll our tongues," Molly said. They both stuck their tongues out to demonstrate. "Can you roll yours?" she asked.

Alan shook his head and stuck his tongue out, laughing as it wiggled around but didn't fold. "You must get that from your mother," he told Molly.

"I can't do it either," Iris said. "But . . . I can wiggle my ears! Bet you can't do that," she challenged.

Molly tried, but her head just moved back and forth.

"I can do it!" Bailey exclaimed, pushing her hair behind her ears and showing them.

She knew it! Bailey was hers. All these things couldn't be a coincidence. There were no traces of Sasha in the child. At first, she'd assumed that Bailey got her coloring from Sasha, but the truth was that Iris and Sasha both had dark hair and olive complexions. Sasha's eyes were blue, and Bailey's were brown—like hers. Okay, also like Donny's, but still. The connection she felt to Bailey was more than just affection for a friend of her stepdaughter's. She thought back to her last in vitro cycle and the day of her transfer. Donny had gone with her, of course, and they'd waited for Sasha to come and tell her how many embryos were viable.

"I wish I had better news," Sasha told her, her eyes full of what Iris had thought was compassion at the time, but now knew was deception. "Only two embryos are viable, and we like to see an eight-cell for the best chances of implantation. Yours are both six cells."

Iris looked at Donny, and he looked away. At the time she'd chalked it up to his being disappointed, but now she knew that it was because he and Sasha were already sleeping together. He was probably glad that her chances were low.

"I don't understand. When you did the egg retrieval, you said you got six eggs. Only two of those fertilized, even with ICSI?" Iris asked.

Sasha pursed her lips and shrugged. "We can only do so much. The rest is up to the universe."

Looking back, Iris now knew that Sasha must have been after Donny from the start. She encouraged him to bring Iris in as a patient so she could sabotage her pregnancy. And worse than that, she had stolen Iris's embryos and had them implanted in herself. Her mind was racing as she fed the girls their pancakes and pondered her next move. She studied Bailey as she ate, watching the way she chewed, the expression on her face, the tone of her voice. This was her daughter. She was positive. Sasha had stolen not only her husband but her child too. And one thing was for damn sure: Iris was getting

76

her back.

After Bailey went home, Iris told Alan she was going out to pick up a few things from the store. Instead she went to a local coffee shop and took out her laptop. Bringing up a search engine, she typed: *Cases of stolen embryos.*

The page was populated with articles. She clicked on one citing a lawsuit against a fertility clinic and read with horror about a couple whose embryo had been sold and implanted in another woman in South America. She clicked on the next article, about a lawsuit initiated by a couple who had been told their embryos had all been used, only to be contacted twenty years later and told that two were found "lost" in a storage facility. The next link detailed a couple who gave birth to twins, only to be contacted by the clinic after their birth and told the wrong embryos had been implanted in them, and they had to give the children up. The knot in her stomach grew as she read story after story of mismanagement, minimal oversight of fertility facilities, and out-and-out criminal activity. These kinds of things were not one in a million, sadly, but all too common. She closed her laptop and hurried to her car, her hand shaking as she pulled out her phone and called her sister.

"Hey there," Violet answered.

"When are you coming back?" Violet had been in New York for the past two weeks for business meetings.

"I was supposed to come back tomorrow, but the merger is taking longer than we expected, and I'll be at least another week. Everything okay?"

"Promise not to think I'm crazy."

"Oookay . . ."

"You know how Bailey's been spending a lot of time with us, right? Well, she's allergic to berries like me, and she has a lot of my mannerisms, and we both love mint chocolate chip ice cream. She has a mole in the same spot I do. She can wiggle her ears. I think . . . I think she's my daughter."

She waited for Violet to talk, but there was silence on the line.

"Vi? Are you there?"

"Yes, I'm just trying to think of what to say. Iris, you do realize that sounds . . . sorry, but . . . crazy."

"I know how it sounds. But listen, it happens. Embryos *are* stolen, put in the wrong person. She was my fertility doctor. She handled my embryos. What was to stop her from changing the name on them to hers and having them implanted?"

"I mean, I don't know. But why would she do that? Why would she want to *take* your child? That makes no sense."

"Don't you see? She wanted Donny, and if *I* got pregnant, then he wouldn't leave me. But if she were pregnant . . ."

"Okay, but why not just destroy your embryos, or damage them, and get pregnant with her own egg? Or naturally. She is younger. That seems like a really out-there thing to do to get a guy."

"I'm telling you. I feel a connection to Bailey. I can't explain it, it's something I've never felt before, but I know it in my bones."

"Honey, I don't know what to say. What can you do? There's no way to know, and I don't mean to be insensitive, but you did go

78

through a deep depression after everything. Are you sure it's not just being around Donny and her again that's bringing up all the old stuff? I want to support you, but I just don't see how what you're saying could be true."

"I have to know."

"How?"

"I have a plan."

"Please, wait until I'm home and we can talk through this? Don't do anything rash."

"I won't. Please keep this between us."

"Of course."

She ended the call, opened the saved website on her phone, and placed the order she'd been considering in the back of her mind for weeks. Bailey was her child, and she was going to prove it.

# Chapter Fourteen
## Sasha

Sasha stormed into the house, calling out for Donny, who, for once, was home before she was. Angela greeted her and pointed outside.

"He's with Bailey on the deck."

Sasha sighed and blew out an exasperated breath. "Well, I need to speak to him privately. Would you please take Bailey upstairs and get her ready for bed?" It was only six o'clock, but too bad.

Angela didn't argue, just nodded and walked outside to retrieve Bailey.

"Hi, Mommy!" Bailey ran up and gave her a hug. Sasha patted her head absentmindedly, her focus entirely on the conversation she needed to have with her husband. "Hi, honey. Run along, and I'll be up to tuck you in soon."

"It's too early for bed," Bailey whined.

"Just get ready and have Angela read to you. I'll be up in a little."

"I can read to myself," she muttered as she stomped away.

Sasha opened the French doors and walked to the far end of the deck where Donny sat drinking a scotch and scrolling through his phone.

"She's really done it this time!" Sasha didn't bother with a greeting.

He looked up, his brows creased. "Who?"

"Your ex! She complained to the headmistress that Ms. Kelly

was hindering Bailey's reading potential. I had to hear about it from Melanie, who happened to be late picking up her daughter, Denim, and overheard the whole conversation."

"Denim?" Donny said, a smile tugging at his lips.

"That's what you're choosing to focus on? Iris has no business talking to the teacher about *our* daughter. She's way overstepping. I told you it was a bad idea to let the girls spend so much time together. Bailey's over there almost every day now!"

Sasha reached over and grabbed his glass of scotch, downing the rest in one swallow.

"Okay, calm down. I need a little more context. Why did Iris think the teacher was interfering with Bailey's potential?"

Sasha gave him an exasperated look. "Something about her telling Bailey the book she chose was too hard. And Bailey having to prove to her that she could read it."

"Well, I don't like the sound of that. Why would her teacher do that?"

"Are you serious? That's not the point! Why is Iris going to the teacher on Bailey's behalf? It's none of her damn business, and if she's really so concerned, she should have called me."

He arched a brow but said nothing.

"What?"

"I don't know, maybe she didn't think you'd be receptive to her calling you."

"Are you going to say something to her, or what? She needs to be put in her place, and I shouldn't have to be the one to do it. Don't you agree that what she did was totally inappropriate?"

"Maybe, I just don't want to overreact. Iris has always been passionate about books, so she was probably just upset when Bailey told her what happened. Why don't you talk to the teacher and get the full story? Maybe Iris was there about Molly, and she happened to mention it."

He might be right. Melanie *was* a gossip and tended to exaggerate. Sasha decided she'd call the school tomorrow. The thing that bugged her the most was that Bailey had told Iris about it, not her. Why wouldn't Bailey complain to *her* mom about this teacher? Sasha certainly would have put the teacher in her place. After all, they weren't paying thousands of dollars a year for her daughter to get a subpar education. If anything, the teacher should be encouraging them to read *above* their reading level, not be blasé about maintaining the status quo. "Okay, you're right. It just upset me, that's all. You know how much I love Bailey. I only want to protect her."

"Of course."

Just when her equilibrium had been restored, Bailey came tearing outside, holding a book and waving it at Sasha.

"Mommy, you said you'd come up! I want you to tuck me in and read a good night prayer with me."

"A what?" Sasha said.

Bailey plopped the book down on the table next to Sasha. "A prayer. Good night prayers. Molly says them every night, and when I said I didn't know how, Mommy Iris bought a book for me."

"*Mommy* Iris?" Sasha shrieked. "Who told you to call her that? You little brat!"

Bailey's lip began to tremble, and she ran to Donny, who opened his arms and held her.

"Sasha!" Donny gasped.

"Look at me. Now!" Sasha commanded. "Did Iris tell you to call her that?"

Bailey looked up, a tear rolling down her cheek. "It was my idea. I did it to help Molly."

"Don't you lie to me . . ."

"Stop," Donny said. He put his hand on Bailey's chin. "It's okay, sweetie. What do you mean, you did it to help Molly?"

"She's really sad and misses her mommy who died. Iris is a good mommy to her, and she wants to love her like a mommy, but she's afraid that her real mommy will be sad. I told her maybe it would be okay to call her Mommy Iris and that I would too, since we're like sisters."

Donny gave Sasha a look that made her want to punch him in the face. He was buying this bullshit. Bailey was good—she'd give her that. She made herself look like a little angel when in fact she was a spoiled brat who didn't care about hurting her own mommy's feelings. But Donny was too smitten with his little girl to see that, and Sasha was not about to let him see *her* in a bad light.

"I'm sorry for yelling at you, sweetie. That was very kind of you. But you already have a mommy, so you don't need to call her Mommy Iris, okay? Just the way Molly doesn't need to call me

Mommy Sasha," she said in a sugary-sweet tone.

Bailey glared at her. "She wouldn't call you Mommy Sasha. She doesn't know you."

Donny stood and scooped Bailey in his arms. "Okay, I think it's time for bed. Why don't I read one of those prayers with you?"

But Sasha stood up and blocked him. "No, no. I'll do it. Bailey asked me to. It'll be a nice mother-daughter routine."

Donny put Bailey down and Sasha reached for her hand, which Bailey reluctantly took. As they walked away, Sasha squeezed it a little harder than necessary, willing herself to appear calm. She'd say the prayers with Bailey tonight, but the book would go missing after that. Then she'd take Bailey to the store to pick out a new one—one that they chose together.

They went upstairs and she read the prayer that Bailey had chosen. "Okay, time for bed now. And remember, you only have one mommy."

"Okay. I'm sorry."

"You should be. How would you like it if I told Denim to call me Mommy?" Sasha knew that Demin, the most popular girl in Bailey's class, wasn't always kind to Bailey. Not that she was a bully or anything, but Bailey just wasn't quite in her league. And even though Sasha had prodded Bailey repeatedly to take more care with her appearance, she refused to put the ribbons that Sasha bought in her hair, or to wear the darling outfits Sasha would put out for playdates. So, it was her own fault, really, that she wasn't always included in Demin's circle.

Bailey's eyes were as big as saucers. "Denim's not nice. I don't want her to be my sister."

"Well, see. Iris isn't so nice to me, and I don't want her to be your mommy."

Bailey frowned. "Iris *is* nice!"

"Ugh." Sasha stood. "Fine. Just remember what I said."

When Sasha returned downstairs, Donny was waiting for her in the living room.

"*Now* do you see why I'm not happy with her being around Molly so much? Mommy Iris. What in the actual . . ." She shook her head. "I've seen this before, you know."

"Seen what?"

"An infertile woman becoming overinvolved with someone else's child. Maybe because Bailey is yours and she used to be married to you, she thinks she has some kind of connection to her. Bailey told me that she gave her some of her old Nancy Drew books. Why wouldn't she save them for Molly? Now she's having our daughter call her Mommy! Something's off here. I don't want to find out one day that she disappeared with our daughter."

"Sasha! Come on. That's a bit dramatic, don't you think? She's been through a lot, but she's not crazy."

"I'm not so sure. You may play a fertility doc on TV, but this is my area of expertise. You'd be surprised at the lengths some women will go to satisfy their maternal urges."

"Look, I'll admit the Mommy Iris thing is weird. But you heard Bailey, it was her idea. She was being a good friend, that's all."

"You're so naïve. Don't you see that Iris could have manipulated her into thinking that?"

He threw his hands up. "I don't know what to say. Iris is happy now. She has her own family."

"Now that you mention that . . . I wonder. How did Alan's wife die?"

"What?"

"Wasn't it some kind of accident? And then he's dating Iris six months later. Maybe she had something to do with it. If she couldn't have her own child, she would find someone else's."

The look of horror on his face let her know she'd gone too far. She shook her head. "Of course I don't mean that. But I wonder if she did marry him more because of his daughter than because of him. You heard Bailey—Molly still misses her mother and hasn't really accepted Iris in that role. What if now she's moving on to Bailey? I'm scared, Donny."

"Wow. You really think that's possible?"

Finally, she had an opening. "Yes. Women get desperate. I think we need to get Bailey away from Iris. Maybe we should move her from Beardsley-Arms. I mean, this whole thing with the reading . . ."

"I don't disagree that some distance from Iris would be good, but Beardsley is the best school around here."

"Maybe we should consider boarding school? There are some amazing ones."

"Boarding school? But she's so young!"

"Bailey is so bright. I think she needs more than she's getting here. Don't you want her to have the best chance to succeed in life? Denim's mom is going to send her to boarding school next year, you know. She's done all the research and was telling me about it at lunch the other day, how these schools prepare their students to excel. They teach discipline and a sense of responsibility. There are fewer distractions and children do much better academically."

She kept going, working every possible angle. "You're always working, and my practice is so demanding. Angela spends more time with Bailey than we do. Why not let her be in an environment that can offer more than a babysitter? They have equestrian lessons, art appreciation, music. All sorts of extras you don't find in a day school."

"I don't know, Sash. Wouldn't you miss her?"

"Of course," she said. "But it's a parent's job to put the welfare of their children above what *they* want. I think it could be a wonderful advantage for her. Let's at least think about it. She could transfer after the holidays. I'm concerned that she's becoming too attached to Iris. It's not healthy. I told you how unhinged infertility can make women."

He nodded. "I can't argue with that. It does seem like Iris is becoming too focused on her. Let me think about it."

Sasha wanted Iris out of their lives, and most particularly out of Bailey's life. She was too close, and it scared her. It was clear that Donny harbored no ill will toward his ex-wife. After the birthday party he admitted that he felt guilty about the way he'd ended his marriage to Iris. She wasn't about to let the friendship between their daughters be the vehicle that allowed Iris back into Donny's world. Never. That could completely upend her life.

# Chapter Fifteen
## Iris

Iris was about to leave to pick up Molly from school when her phone rang. She was surprised to see Donny's number come up.

"Hello?"

"Hi, Iris, do you have a minute?" he said, his voice smooth and deep, and Iris was, for a moment, thrown back in time.

Recovering, she replied. "Uh, sure. I'm on my way to get Molly. What's up?"

"Um, this is awkward, but I'm calling because Sasha and I have some concerns. Bailey referred to you as Mommy Iris, and Sasha hit the roof."

"Oh, I'm so sorry! It wasn't my idea, Donny."

"I know, I know. Bailey explained. But that's not all. We found out that you talked to their teacher about Bailey's reading . . . ? Anyway, we don't think it's a good idea for Bailey to go to your house anymore. If the girls have a playdate, it has to be at our house."

Iris gripped the phone tighter. She couldn't let this happen. Not until she found out the truth. "I'm so sorry. I didn't mean to interfere. I was there to talk about Molly, and it just came up. I should have never said anything about Bailey." Actually, she used Molly as a pretext to make sure that the woman didn't dampen Bailey's enthusiasm for reading. Iris knew how important it was to nurture a child's passion for learning, and that a bad teacher could do more damage than most people realized.

"Oh, well, I thought that might be it. Still, you need to be more careful. This situation is . . . fraught."

She wanted to point out that he was the one who created this "situation," but she couldn't afford to alienate him right now. "I'm happy to apologize to Sasha if that would help. Molly would be heartbroken if she couldn't see Bailey."

"That's not necessary. I'll relay your apologies. And they can still see each other, but as I said, it'll have to be at our house."

"Wait, Donny. This Saturday is the anniversary of Molly's mother's accident. I really want to help her get through the day. She's been looking forward to having Bailey over all week. She's planned the whole night, they're putting on a play with Oscar. It has to be at our house. Can you please let her come just one more time?" It wasn't true, but she had to play on his sympathies. Hopefully neither of them would find out she was lying.

She heard him sigh. "Oh, I didn't realize. Let me talk to Sasha, and I'll get back to you."

"Thank you, Donny. It would mean the world to her. And to me."

\* \* \*

This was her last chance. They'd all just finished watching *Mulan*, and the girls were brushing their teeth. Iris walked into the bathroom to check on them.

"Good job, girls. Who wants to play a game?"

"I do!" they both answered.

Iris pulled out two Q-tips. "It's called the giggle game. Whoever doesn't laugh when I tickle their cheek with this is the winner."

"Me first!" Molly cried.

"Okay, open wide." Iris swabbed the inside of her cheek, and she burst into giggles. Iris put the Q-tip in her pocket.

"I'm gonna win!" Bailey opened her mouth next, and Iris repeated the procedure as Bailey looked straight ahead, trying hard to be serious. "I won!"

As Iris was finishing up, she heard footsteps and spun around to see Alan standing there, a confused expression on his face.

"What are you doing?" he whispered, staring at the Q-tip still in her hand. She dropped it in her pocket.

"Girls, go on to Molly's room. I'll be there soon."

"But I won," Bailey said.

"Yes, sweetie, you did. Run along and I'll be in to tuck you both in." After they'd gone, she turned back to Alan. "Let's go to our room."

She shut the door behind them and braced herself for his questions.

"Iris, were you swabbing Bailey's cheek? What's going on?"

"Bailey is my daughter, and I'm going to prove it!"

He looked at her as though she'd lost her mind. "What? How can you say that?" Alan knew all about her infertility and that Sasha had been her doctor.

"I know she stole my embryo. It all makes sense now. She's so cold to Bailey. I think she did it just to break up my marriage. She doesn't even care about being a mother!"

Alan took her hand in his. "Honey, I know what you went through was horrible. And I can't even imagine the sense of betrayal you felt at having your husband leave you for Sasha, after you put all your trust in her. But this is too much. Sasha might not be the model mother, but you can't say she doesn't care about Bailey just because she has a nanny. Lots of women do."

She shook her head. "It's not that. Bailey's starved for attention. From what she's told me, even when Sasha is home, she has no time or interest in her. She treats Bailey like one of her accessories."

He didn't look convinced. "So what's your plan? A DNA test? You can't do that without her parents' permission, you know."

"I just need to know the truth. I'll worry about the legalities later. If I'm wrong, no one will ever know. But if I'm right, then she's the one who needs to worry about the law. Please try to understand."

"I'm sorry, but I can't go along with this. It's not right. If someone did that to Molly, I'd be outraged. Give me the Q-tip."

"No," she said, turning away from him.

"Iris, come on. You have to be rational. I know how badly you wanted to be a mother. And you are a mother to Molly. You have to let this go. It's not good for you."

"Fine, you win." She sighed and reached into her pocket and gave him the Q-tip.

"Thank you. And I think it's best if we suspend these sleepovers for a while. Molly will understand."

"You're right. I probably need some distance from the situation." She didn't tell him that tonight was the last night Donny and Sasha were allowing Bailey to come over anyway. Let him think he had persuaded her that she was wrong.

"I'm going to brush my teeth," she said as she went into their bathroom. She reached into her pocket and pulled out the remaining Q-tip. She'd bent the end of the one Molly used so she'd be able to tell them apart. She put Bailey's swab into a plastic bag and hid it in one of the vanity drawers. Tomorrow she'd send it to the lab to be compared with a swab she'd taken from her own cheek. She'd done her research and found a company that performed mitochondrial DNA tests tracing a person's matrilineal line—mtDNA passed from a mother to all her children. The fascinating thing about mtDNA was that it never changed. So if you compared the mtDNA of someone who lived one thousand years ago to that of a direct descendant living today, it would be a perfect match. She filled the form using Molly's name instead of Bailey's, signing off as a legal guardian. Once she mailed it, all she had to do was wait.

# Chapter Sixteen
## Sasha

In the back of her mind, Sasha still worried that Margo would tell Ian everything and Donny would find out the truth. She thought she'd never see her again once she left Georgia. They had been best friends once—before the night that changed everything. She hadn't thought about it in years. But she went back there now, to that hot summer night so many years ago when she was young and free and the world seemed safe. She and Margo were only seventeen, but they looked much older. Sasha's mother was working the late shift, and Margo's parents were away for the weekend, so they didn't need to worry about curfew. The bar they snuck into was known to look the other way, so when they'd pretend to forget their IDs at home, the bartender would serve them anyway. Sasha was always the more adventurous of the two, and it was her idea to try and sneak in to see their favorite local band, Rollercoaster. She could still remember how the bar smelled of beer and cheap perfume. She and Margo were perched on their bar stools near the front of the bar, where they had a front-row view of the band. She didn't know how many beers they had before they were off their seats and on the crowded dance floor, moving their bodies seductively in front of the band members. Sasha caught the eye of the drummer, Bobby, who winked at her, and she flushed with delight. When the band took a break, the cute drummer came up and whispered in her ear.

"You girls wanna party when we're finished?"

She tried to sound blasé when she shrugged and said, "Sounds cool."

When the band started up again and she and Margo were back at the bar, two shots appeared in front of them.

"Compliments of Bobby," the bartender said, inclining his head toward the stage.

By the time two a.m. rolled around, Sasha was having a hard time walking, but she didn't let that stop her from going with Bobby and the other three band members in their van. Margo was giggling as she stumbled, and the girls helped each other arm in arm until they were seated and the van took off.

"Where are we going?" Margo asked, slurring her words.

"To party, baby," one of the other guys said. A few minutes later they arrived at a motel.

Sasha stopped before they went inside. Something didn't feel right. "I wanna go home."

Bobby looked at her with contempt. "Are you kidding me? We coulda had our pick of any girls tonight. Now you wanna leave?"

"Yeah, come on, Susan. It was your idea to come out tonight. Don't be a baby now," Margo said, smiling at Davey, the guitarist.

Sasha could see Margo was still trying to act cool. She gave her a beseeching look. "I think we should go."

"Do what you want, but I'm going to party with these guys."

Sasha didn't want to leave her alone, so she followed her inside.

"Grab a seat and we'll get some drinks," Davey said.

Sasha plopped down on the threadbare sofa and put her head in her hands, willing herself not to be sick. Margo was dancing around the living room to the music, making Sasha dizzy just looking at her. Bobby came over and handed her a red Solo cup, took a seat next to her, and slung his arm around her shoulder.

"This will make you feel better. It's ginger ale."

She took it from him and drank. "Thanks."

She continued to sip it, hoping to quell the nausea. She watched as Margo disappeared into the bedroom with Davey and the door shut. She finished the drink and closed her eyes. She felt the cushion next to her move and opened her eyes to see Bobby next to her. He put an arm around her and massaged her shoulder.

"You're so beautiful. I couldn't keep my eyes off you all night," he whispered.

She felt herself blush, flattered and nervous that this cool older guy thought she was special. He leaned in to kiss her and she let him. Soon they were tangled up together on the sofa and things progressed too quickly for her to catch her breath. When it was over, he fell asleep, and she ran into the bathroom and threw up. What had she just done? And with no protection. What if she got pregnant? She returned to the sofa and tried to sleep but lay there until the sun finally came up, then jumped up and banged on the bedroom door.

"Margo. We have to go. I told my mom I'd be home in the morning. She thinks I'm at your house!"

The door opened, and Margo stumbled out, seeming to be half out of it. "Okay, let me find my purse."

Bobby drove them to Margo's house, and Sasha walked home

from there. It was another year before she found out what that night had cost her.

If Margo didn't keep her promise to her and told Ian about what happened all those years ago, it could ruin her. She wasn't sure she could trust Margo to keep her word, but what choice did she have? And there was no way she could tell Margo the truth. She would just have to hope that her former friend meant it when she'd promised to have her back. In the meantime, she would come up with a contingency plan. Sasha had worked too hard to get everything she wanted. She wasn't about to let anyone take it away from her.

# Chapter Seventeen
## Iris

It had been an agonizing ten days for Iris, not being able to see Bailey and waiting for the results of the DNA test. She couldn't concentrate on her work, she was short with Alan, and she couldn't help but replay every memory from her last IVF cycle over and over, trying to figure out if there was anything she might have missed to tip her off to what had happened.

She opened her laptop, and her heart skipped a beat when she saw she had an email from the lab. Her hand shook as she moved her mouse and clicked on it. Her eyes scanned the message and she sat back in her chair, shaken. Blood pounded in her ears as she absorbed the news. Bailey's mitochondrial DNA was a perfect match to hers.

She was right! Bailey *was* her daughter! Elation filled her at the news that she was a mother. But her joy was short-lived as the implications of what Sasha had done hit her. Not only had she stolen her child and kept her from Iris for seven years—she'd stolen her hope, her self-confidence, part of her identity as a woman. Then she wondered, had Donny known? Could he have been complicit in this atrocity Sasha had committed? She doubled over in pain, her breath coming faster, and thought she would be sick. Sweat broke out on her forehead, and she breathed in and out, trying to calm down. What should she do next?

Violet. She needed to talk to Violet. She'd gotten home from New York late last night and was taking the day off today. Iris printed the email, grabbed her purse, and ran out the door.

It took her twenty minutes to reach her sister's house in Inglewood. Her heart was still racing as she parked and ran up the walkway to the large ranch house. She tapped her foot as she rang the bell, feeling like she would burst out of her skin. Violet appeared, looked out in surprise and opened the door all the way.

"Hey. What's going on?"

"Sorry to drop in on you, but we need to talk."

They went into the kitchen, and Iris sat down at the round table, drumming her fingers, waiting for Violet to join her.

"Coffee?" she asked as she poured from the pot into a mug.

Iris shook her head.

Violet sat across form her. "Okay, what is it? Are you okay?"

Iris pulled the paper form her purse and took a deep breath. "Hear me out. I had a DNA test done on Bailey."

"What?" Violet interrupted. "Iris, I thought we agreed you'd back off."

"Don't you want to know the results?"

Violet's eyes widened. "No!"

"Yes!" She thrust the paper into her sister's hands.

"Oh my . . . but how? She's really your daughter? Are you sure?"

Iris explained about the mtDNA. "There's no mistake. Sasha *stole* my child!"

Violet sprang up from her seat and began to pace. "This is unbelievable! And Donny . . . do you think he knew?"

"I've been going over it and over it, and as much as I hate what he did to me, I can't believe he would go along with something this diabolical."

"You need to talk to a lawyer."

"I will, but . . . I didn't exactly get the results legally. You need parental consent. I put Molly's name on the test."

"Still, what matters is the truth. And what she did . . . I can't imagine if someone had taken Maggie or Matt from me." She teared up. "I'm so sorry for not believing you. Can you forgive me?"

"Of course. I know you were only worried about me."

"This must be killing you. I'd want to go and grab her right now."

"I do too, but I think kidnapping is frowned upon." She surprised even herself with her gallows humor. "I think I have to go to Donny."

Violet shook her head. "I don't know. What if he *did* know?"

"I think it's a chance I'm going to have to take. I need him on my side. He's a decent person. I think he'll do the right thing."

Violet arched an eyebrow. "The right thing? Like leaving you for your fertility doctor?"

"You know what I mean. He may have cheated on me, but he would never go along with something like this. He loves Bailey, she talks about him all the time. He must see how cold Sasha is to her. And now it makes sense. Bailey isn't hers. She must hate her in some ways, knowing I'm her real mother."

"This is beyond horrendous. How can someone do something like this? You trusted her." She put her hands on her hips. "I'll tell you one thing. She's going down. She's going to lose her license. I promise you, I will do everything in my power to make her pay."

Iris smiled at her sister. "I know you will. You've always looked out for me."

"No one messes with my little sister," she said in a brave voice, but Iris could see she was struggling not to cry.

"Okay, I'm going home, and then I'll call Donny. I'll keep you posted."

"Are you sure you don't want to talk to an attorney first?"

"Yeah. If I don't get anywhere with Donny, then that'll be my next step. But I'm sure he's not going to want this kind of scandal splashed all over the news. If he doesn't help me, I'll get a lawyer and file a claim to compel the court to do their own test. But that could take time, and I don't want to have this drag out in family court."Okay. Please be careful."

"Don't worry, I'll be fine."

"Worry is my middle name," Violet said as she pulled her in for a tight hug.

Iris got behind the wheel and pulled out her phone. Pulling up Donny's contact, she texted him: *Need to see you asap. Urgent. Can't wait.*

Her phone pinged back seconds later. *What's wrong?*

She responded. *Not over text. Meet me at the Pier, our old spot, 6:00 pm. After everything you've done— you owe me a few minutes of your time.* Donny had always been susceptible to guilt. And anyway, he did owe her.

*See you then* was his response.

T minus eight hours before she set the wheels in motion to reclaim her daughter.

# Chapter Eighteen
## Sasha

Sasha was enjoying a home massage after a long day dealing with emotional women. She didn't understand how anyone could become so obsessed with procreating. It was fortunate for her, of course. Her clientele could afford to pay tens of thousands of dollars on cycle after cycle. But even those who weren't rich and famous would exhaust their life savings to try and achieve the dream of becoming parents. Sasha had never wanted to be a mother. She'd made the sacrifice for Donny, but the truth was, she regretted it. Bailey was a drain on his time and attention, and constantly needed affirmation, approval, accolades. She was a self-centered little pest. But at least soon she'd be away at boarding school, and Sasha would only have to put up with her on holidays. She'd find a nice sleepaway camp for the summers.

The masseuse finished up, and Sasha stretched languidly, feeling more relaxed than she had all week. Angela had put Bailey to bed an hour before, and the house was deliciously quiet. Donny had texted her that he had a last-minute meeting with the director and would be home sometime after seven. She took a long shower, then changed into a silky robe over the bustier she'd bought earlier that day. Her campaign to drive Donny mad with lust was in full swing. She needed every possible advantage until the little brat was firmly ensconced three thousand miles away at her new school.

It was eight o'clock and Donny still wasn't home. She was pouring herself a second glass of wine when she heard the front door chime and she looked up to see him walking toward her. He looked strange. His face was flushed, and his eyes were narrowed. As he got closer, she could see that he was angry.

"How could you?" he yelled.

"What?"

"I just saw Iris. What kind of a monster are you?"

She froze.

He looked down the hall. "Where's Bailey? I don't want her to overhear."

"She's sleeping."

"Come with me down to the beach."

"Give me a minute to change." She went upstairs and pulled on a pair of jeans and a sweater. Back downstairs, she followed him out on the deck, trying to maintain a facade of composure. He'd met with Iris?

Once they reached the beach, he began walking furiously away from the house.

"Donny, what is going on?" she called, frantically struggling to keep pace with him.

He stopped suddenly and whirled around to face her, tears of fury in his eyes. "I didn't believe her at first, didn't want to. I gave up everything for you. I thought you were special. I ended my marriage, blew up my life, because you convinced me that you were carrying our child. But you lied. You stole. What kind of a person does that?"

"I don't know what you're talking about," she lied.

He balled his hands into tight fists, and for a minute she wondered if he was going to hit her. "You know exactly what I'm talking about. Bailey is Iris's daughter. You implanted her embryo into you."

She feigned shock. "Do you hear yourself? That's ridiculous. Where would you get an idea like that?"

He pulled a piece of paper from his pocket. "From Iris. Here are the results of the DNA test."

Her stomach dropped. She grabbed the paper and scanned it. "But this test says Molly."

"Molly isn't related to her. She just used her name because she's her legal guardian."

"How dare she take a DNA test of *our* daughter without our permission. I'll sue her."

He started laughing then, a maniacal cackle. "You'll sue *her*? You were her doctor, and you stole her embryos. You're worried about what *she* did?"

She had to think of something to say. Damn nosy Iris. She never should have allowed Bailey over there. "That test won't hold up in court. It was obtained illegally."

"Do you think I care about what happens in court? Do you know what this is going to do to Bailey? What the hell is wrong with you? We have to do the right thing. Bailey is *her* daughter. This has to be set right. And you are never going to practice medicine again, do you understand that?"

"Donny, please listen to me. I did it for you. For us. We were in love, and if she'd gotten pregnant, you wouldn't have left her. We belong together."

"Are you kidding me? You're actually justifying this? You of all people know the emotional toll infertility takes on a woman, on a marriage. What you did is unforgivable."

She started to cry. "I do know, actually. I can't have children. I'm infertile. I wanted to give you a child, and that was the only way I could do it."

He looked at her with hate in his eyes. "What are you talking about? I don't understand."

"All I wanted was you. Iris was selfish. When I asked about using a surrogate, you told me that she refused because she wanted to carry her own child. Don't you see how much more I loved you? I was willing to bear someone else's child—raise her as my own—just to be with you!"

"You're crazy. We're over. I'm filing for divorce, and Iris and I are going to a lawyer. I'm ordering a new DNA test so that it's all legal, and I'm filing for an immediate injunction so that you can't go near my daughter. And you'll never practice medicine again when we're through with you. Hopefully, you'll go to prison as well."

Sasha knew when to concede defeat. There was no way she was going to regain Donny's trust. But there was no way in hell she was going to prison or losing her medical license, either. "If you try to do that, I'll fight you. I'll say I was undergoing IVF at the time I met you because I'm infertile. I can make the records reflect that. And just in case you care at all—*I'm* the victim. I was seduced by an older guy, some scumbag in a band, when I was only seventeen. I found out later he gave me chlamydia, but I didn't know, and it went untreated. Both my tubes were too scarred for me to get pregnant. All of these rich, prissy women I treat all day, the Irises, they think have it so bad. They have no idea."

Donny was quiet, seeming to look at her with compassion. Maybe she could fix this after all.

"Well, I'm sorry to hear that, but that's no excuse, Sasha. What you did is . . . I don't even have words for how horrible it is. You need to be punished."

She always knew this day might come and had already thought about how she would protect herself. "I'll say I must have mistakenly mixed up the embryos. You'll never be able to prove it was intentional."

"You are vile," he said, shaking his head.

"Here's how this is going to go. We'll say this was all a mix-up. I'll give up my claim on custody, and Iris can have her brat back. We tell Bailey that it was just a big mistake, and that Daddy and Mommy are getting divorced. I keep my license. There's no scandal splashing your face across the cover of *People* magazine. And you give me half of everything."

"I'm not giving you a cent. You deserve to rot in prison."

She played her trump card. "You may not realize this, but the law hasn't quite caught up with science yet. Since *I* gave birth to Bailey, you'll still have to fight me for custody. That can be a long process, and in the meantime, I'll poison her against you. She'll hate you by the time I'm finished. I suggest you do as I say if you want to protect your precious little brat."

He leaned in close to her, his eyes slits. "Fine," he spat. "Half of everything is a small price to get rid of you. But I want you out of the house, tonight. Go to the Four Seasons or something. I never want to have to see you again. From now on, we only speak through the divorce lawyers."

She nodded and walked back to the house ahead of him. It wasn't how she wanted things to turn out, but for a small-town girl from Dalton, Georgia, half of Donny's millions wasn't bad. And she was still young enough and certainly attractive enough to pick herself up—the ex-wife of Donny McBride would be a hot ticket. She'd have a new lover in no time. As a matter of fact, she had a new patient with an extremely attractive husband who was a big-time producer. There was definitely potential.

# Chapter Nineteen
## Iris

*One Year Later*

Bailey and Molly splashed in the pool while Alan and Iris sat at a nearby table sipping iced tea, Oscar at their feet chewing on a bone.

"Mommy, watch me do a dive," Molly said. Putting her arms together and aiming her head toward the pool, she sprang off the board and sliced the water with her hands. When she surfaced, Iris clapped.

"Wonderful! Definitely a ten."

Molly gave her a broad smile.

"My turn, Mommy," Bailey said. "Watching?"

"Yes, darling. Go on."

Bailey bounced three times, then executed a perfect dive into the deep end. Again, Iris clapped.

"Another ten! You two are practically turning into fish."

The girls giggled and swam together to the shallow end, where they took turns doing somersaults and grading each other. Iris's heart swelled as she watched them, still in awe that she was their mother. There were times she woke up in the middle of the night and tiptoed into their bedroom to make sure it wasn't all a dream.

They had come a long way in the past year, and it hadn't been easy. Bailey had been understandably traumatized. No matter how bad a mother Sasha was, she was the only mother Bailey knew. Donny and Iris wouldn't allow Sasha unsupervised visits with Bailey, for obvious reasons, but they couldn't hurt Bailey by cutting her off all at once. Sasha played her part well, acting as if she still cared for Bailey, but assuring her that she belonged with her real mommy and that in time, she would come to love Iris. It hadn't taken long for Sasha's interest in Bailey to wane, however, after she moved on from Donny and broke up another marriage. Bailey put on a brave face, but Iris knew the rejection hurt her.

Molly had been confused too. As much as she wanted a sister, it was hard for her to come to terms with the fact that Iris was Bailey's real mother, not a stepmother, and she felt like it wasn't fair that Bailey had both her mommies while Molly's was gone. Both girls had suffered tremendous loss in their young lives, but lots of therapy, love, and time were helping them come to terms with it. No one looking at this happy family on a beautiful Saturday would be able to guess at how difficult a road it had been.

She knew that it killed Sasha to have to play nice, but Donny's lawyer had been meticulous in drafting a divorce agreement that ensured her full compliance. Sasha would never have the opportunity to come crashing back into their lives and spreading her venom. If she refused to toe the line, she had a lot to lose, and she knew it. At first, Iris, in her fury, had been bent on confronting Sasha, telling her to her face how much agony and heartbreak she had caused, but she quickly came to realize that shaming Sasha was impossible. You couldn't make someone without a conscience feel guilty. Although

114

Iris mourned the loss of those seven years with her daughter, she made the decision not to waste any more time wallowing in regrets. What mattered now was that they move forward as a family toward healing and growth.

She had even forgiven Donny, who was a broken man. He would live forever with the guilt of what he'd enabled Sasha to do to Iris and their daughter, even if he'd had no idea about her master plan. It was only his deep love for Bailey that gave him the will to go on. She remembered their last conversation after they met with the lawyers to finalize the papers giving Iris full custody. He walked her to her car and opened the door for her.

"There's nothing I can say to convey how sorry I am about everything. I was such an idiot. I still can't believe it. If I could go back in time and do things differently . . ."

She put a hand up. "No. We have to live with the decisions we make. I'm happy. I have a good marriage and two beautiful daughters. As much as I wish I could have those years back with Bailey, I could never wish Alan and Molly away."

"I get it. But I'll live the rest my life regretting this."

She hoped that one day he would be able to forgive himself and was so glad to see the happiness in his eyes on those weekends he had the girls. She and Alan had decided from the beginning that it would be better for the girls if Donny's weekends included both Bailey and Molly. It was important that they not grow up feeling like they belonged to separate families, but as a blended family all their own. Iris was seeing Donny become more like the man she had first known, and she wished him well. He was the father of her child, and she wanted Bailey to have two parents who were well and happy.

For the first time in her life, Iris felt complete. She had two daughters, and she loved them each fully and equally. She'd even come to be grateful that she'd been adopted because she understood better than anyone that love had nothing to do with blood. Molly was as much her child as Bailey was, and she would lay her life down for either of them. And just as Iris and Violet loved each other as much as any blood sisters, Molly and Bailey felt the same way. Their relationship continued to blossom, and even though they weren't physically related, they were so close that their mannerisms and tones became similar. When they went out, most people assumed that they were biological sisters. When she thought about everything she'd been through to bring her to where she was today, Iris chose to give thanks, that at last the deepest desire of her heart had been fulfilled. She looked over at Alan and smiled.

"Pizza or burgers tonight?"

"Should we let the girls decide?"

Iris nodded. What a joy to only have simple decisions to make. Iris knew that wouldn't always be the case. There would be challenges, heartaches, and bumps in the road. But they would face them together with fortitude and love, and always, always with gratitude.

## THE END

READ ON FOR THE FIRST CHAPTER OF

# THE FIRST SHOT
## A PREQUEL TO THE LAST MRS. PARRISH

# CHAPTER ONE

At three a.m., Lana Crump quietly got out of bed, fully dressed, and slid the suitcase she'd packed earlier that night out from under it. The sound of soft breathing filled the room, and she tiptoed to the crib for a last look at her son, who was sleeping peacefully. She exited the room without a sound. As her feet carried her down the steps and away from the house she'd grown up in, she felt lighter and lighter, thoughts of a better future somewhere far away from this dead-end town filling her head and giving her new purpose.

She'd debated briefly whether or not to leave a note but decided against it. They knew why she had to leave—that she'd never be allowed to raise her son no matter what she did. Taking a final look around, she whispered a quiet goodbye and closed the door behind her.

She'd planned her escape carefully, thinking through every contingency. In her backpack was the emergency cash her mother had kept hidden in the back of the pantry in an old flour canister. A thousand dollars wouldn't get her far, but it was enough for now. She'd already purchased a prepaid cell phone, and she'd be sure to get rid of her real one, sending the police scurrying in the wrong direction. Lastly, she'd packed her copies of *Anna Karenina* and *Persuasion*. She wished she didn't have to leave all of her other books, but there was no other option. Now all she needed to do was hitch a ride to Lexington, Nebraska, where phase two of her plan could begin.

It was close to four a.m. when she reached the bus station and bought a ticket to Little Rock. She hated to squander the $75, but it was the only way. At six fifteen, she handed the driver her ticket and found a seat in the back. She sat down and tucked her phone between the seat cushions, then got back up. As the bus began to fill, she squeezed to the side of an oncoming passenger and snuck off. When they tracked her phone they'd be looking for her in the opposite direction—that would buy her some time. Step one, complete. The sun was coming up as she reached the truck stop and went inside in search of her real ride.

One hour and two cups of coffee later, she was in the passenger seat of an eighteen-wheeler with a trucker named Mac. He was going to Cheyenne but was willing to go a little out of his way to drop her off in Lexington, where she told him she was going to visit her sick aunt. She'd chosen him carefully, after staking out the truck stop all morning to try to get a read on who would be the safest. He had on a wedding band, the first good sign. She'd heard him on the phone talking sweetly to his wife and then his daughter. But the thing that clinched it for her was when he bowed his head before eating to say a silent prayer. It wasn't like she believed all religious people were good, but she had a feeling she'd be safe with Mac.

"How long you planning on staying in Lexington?" he asked as they pulled out.

Lana tried to make herself look sad. "My aunt's pretty sick, so

I'll stay as long she needs me."

"Awful kind of you. Young folks today are usually all about themselves. It's refreshing to see a young woman like you put someone else's needs first."

Lana tried her best not to roll her eyes. Was this do-gooder going to talk the whole way? There was no way she could endure close to five hours of this. She feigned a yawn. "I haven't gotten any sleep since my uncle called to tell me she'd taken a turn for the worse. Would you mind if I just rested for a bit?"

"Of course, of course." He reached behind the seat and pulled a blanket out, handing it to her. "Here you go, try and sleep."

She mumbled a thanks and closed her eyes. Not that she'd really sleep. No matter how nice he seemed, Lana didn't really know him, and she wasn't about to wake up locked in some basement. But as long as she kept her eyes closed, he'd keep his mouth closed. Her old pal Martin Cummings had booked her a room at the Astro Motel for $55 a night—she'd be there behind a locked door soon enough. She had the money for at least a month, but he'd also promised to help her get a job at a local restaurant once they'd squared away her new identity.

Martin hadn't been too thrilled to hear from Lana at first—after all, she was the only one from Blue Springs, Missouri, who knew what he'd done and where'd he gone. Two years ago, she'd been his alibi. He'd been hanging out with the wrong crowd and happened to be in the car with them when they robbed a convenience store in a neighboring town, fatally injuring the clerk. Martin hadn't known what was going to go down, but he'd already had his share of trouble with the law and had begged Lana to cover for him. Just like with her, the cards had always been stacked against Martin, and she was happy to cut him a break. So Lana had been his alibi and told the police he'd been with her that night. Soon after he'd moved away and started a new life. Now he was an integral part of *her* plan to escape. He was working in Eustis, Nebraska, in the vital records department. Thanks to him, she'd have an entirely new identity in no time.

Printed in the USA
CPSIA information can be obtained
at www.ICGtesting.com
LVHW090253151124
796651LV00009B/219

*9780997694253*